PROPERTY OF
FRANKFORT SCHUYLER CENTRAL
HIGH SCHOOL LIBRARY
FRANKFORT, NEW YORK 13340

Swiftwater

Paul Annixter

D1457249

SCHOLASTIC BOOK SERVICES
New York Toronto London Auckland Sydney Tokyo

No part of this publication may be reproduced in whole
or in part, or stored in a retrieval system, or transmitted
in any form or by any means, electronic, mechanical,
photocopying, recording, or otherwise, without written
permission of the publisher. For information regarding
permission, write to Scholastic Book Services, 50 West
44th Street, New York, N.Y. 10036.

ISBN: 0-590-02903-7

*Copyright 1950 by Hill and Wang, Inc. Copyright ©
1960 by TAB Books, Inc. This edition is published by
Scholastic Book Services, a division of Scholastic Maga-
zines, Inc., by arrangement with Hill & Wang, Inc.*

26 25 24 23 22 21 20 19 18 17 16 15   0 1 2 3 4/8

Printed in the U.S.A.

Swiftwater

PROPERTY OF
FRANKFORT SCHUYLER CENTRAL
HIGH SCHOOL LIBRARY
FRANKFORT NEW YORK 13340

PART ONE

1

FOR THREE WEEKS THAT RAINY FALL THE WILD GEESE
lay up in the marshes back of Swiftwater daytimes and
moored out on the lake at night. The little backwoods
settlement got out its shotguns and banged away at the
flock going over, but during the first week not a feather
dropped. The geese only flew a bit higher. They were
used to this sort of enthusiasm the whole length of the
continent. An evening came later, however, during the
shooting, the sky full of the hazy red of an October
sunset, when one of the geese broke formation directly
over the General Store and started a rickety skate toward the beach.

Whit Turner, standing with a group of men and boys,
had just opened his mouth to claim that his shot had
done it when Bucky Calloway crashed his fist into it.
Whit was older and taller, a lanky, raw-boned lad
known to be tough. With his mouth bleeding, he
dropped his shotgun and a fight began. Some of the
men and boys had started toward the shore for the
fallen goose, but the rest stopped to watch. Swiftwater

1

was well represented, in fact—Postmaster Briscoe, Nat Stemline of the General Store, old Doc Waters, and Mr. Dell Fraser, a traveling hardware salesman, who called out with ringside relish: "Let 'em go to it. It'll do 'em both good!"

Dusk thickened as Whit Turner took the beating of his life. He was fighting a young catamount, insensate to pain, and the time came when the best Whit could do was to sit up groggily. The other boy stood over him—white teeth showing, eyes under a shock of unkempt black hair gleaming like a young woods animal's—waiting to make sure his job was finished. Meantime he kept jerking away from a girl now pulling at his bloody hand.

"Oh, Bucky! Why'd you do it? Whatall's come over you?" she kept saying.

"Lemme 'lone, can't you?" the winner gasped, abashed and angry. "I'm sick. I'm goin' home."

He turned and flung away into the dusk.

The interest of Dell Fraser, the hardware salesman, led to questions as the crowd broke up.

"Now that's what I call a high-powered kid," laughed Mr. Fraser. "Did I hear somebody call him Bucky?"

"His name's Bucky Calloway," offered Nat Stemline. "He ain't from this town. He lives up in the woods a piece."

"And who was that slim, stringy-haired girl—his sister?"

"No, that's Bridie Mellott from up on the Shoulder. She and Bucky sort of hold together noticeable."

"What I can't figure is what made him so sore," said the hardware man. "He didn't even fire a shot."

No one seemed positively to know, but old Doc Waters had this to offer: "I believe it was that goose comin' down."

2

"What did he see in that to fight about? He didn't have a gun with him."

"Bucky's different; his father is, too," said Nat Stemline ponderously. " 'Old Never-Stay-Put' we always call Cam Calloway and he's just about as transitory as them wild geese, feels kin to 'em too, they say. Bucky's a piece of the same. This country won't hold either of 'em long, I guess."

"It was the Indians made 'em both queer," elucidated the postmaster. "Father an' son—"

"Indian blood?" Mr. Fraser asked.

"No, but more at home, you might say, in the Indian village than here in town with respectable folk. That was before the Micmacs moved over to the Kennebec Reservation three years ago. Bucky was among 'em a lot as a kid. The Micmac totem, you know, is the wild goose."

"Indian blood nothing," snorted Doane Shattuck, the landman, who had come up. "Cam Calloway and his brood are just fiddle-footed squatters, if you ask me. Plain cracked, too. I ought to know. They're livin' on my land."

There were appreciative snorts from several quarters. "The woods had closed in on the Calloways" was the opinion of most of the townsfolk.

But old Doc Waters said quietly in the silence that followed: "If Cam Calloway's cracked, it's a rift that lets in a patch of sky. I'm here to say it's a pity more of us are not like that."

This was a bit technical perhaps. At any rate a silence followed as the doc moved away in the dark.

The night was misty and unseasonably warm, the shell ice all gone from the lake margin. Alone, down on the beach, Bucky sat listening to the faint gabble of the geese. He'd been hunting for the wounded bird, which no one had found, knowing that even if it was only

3

winged, it would drink itself to death, for that was the proud way of the wounded goose.

Those sounds out there stirred the boy's blood strangely. Always they brought his father close, as if Cam were sitting there right beside him. Goose talk dropping from high sky or riding the lap of the waves, thin and elfin as the voice of the fall wind, keen as heart hunger, haunting as grief or death. It was like Cam's symbol, his totem. His father had said once that a man's soul could vault straight to the high hereafter on a wild goose's call. Whatever could Cam be doing now, Bucky wondered . . . gone off again without a word on one of his strange outjourneys.

At moments a restless ardor flamed in the boy. The misty blackness was like looking down a sooty chimney. There would be intervals of complete silence, except for the lap of the water. He fancied the geese moored out there on the water, taking their long dives for rich tubers among the swaying reeds.

"Must be ten-fifteen foot of water out there where they are," he thought. "Maybe this is their last night here."

Cam would have known about that to the day. Cam could tell just what years the geese would stop here. Bucky could hardly remember when he had first become aware that the wild geese were like the pattern of life—his and Cam's.

Lamed and sore from the fight, he eased his back against a rock. He was sorry about the fight now. There would be hot spots in his chest that wouldn't cool down all summer: one over the way the town would be laughing at him; one over Bridie Mellott's butting in that way. He knew what they'd all be thinking. It was something of that that had come over him at sight of that goose dropping, as if some precious and intimate thing had to be protected, with Cam away and all.

All day he'd been thinking of Cam. As always he felt suffocated in the fear that Cam was gone for good. The core of him seemed muffled in his father's absence. Cam with his magic knowledge of woods, and the weather, and the ways of beasts. Wherever his father was he'd be thinking back home, with the geese talking up like they were tonight.

Almost the first thing he could recall was being awakened in the night by the wild geese out on the lake and in that same night hearing his mother's tearful voice protesting against his father's going away. The sweetish smell of woods-stilled corn whisky was a part of it too. Cam's secret demon.

Another well-polished memory on the same theme . . . Nearly three years ago—he was just coming twelve then —a year before the old Indian village had been cleared out back of Swiftwater. John Silvernail, one of the elderly Micmacs, just drinking enough to awaken the mournful spirit of his tribe, had called him apart from the other boys one day and said: "Bald eagle fly no more—great totem of great people—all come—all go. Big beaver come no more to make dam like no man can do. Big beaver, totem of great people—all come —all go. Wild goose, totem of great people too. Go pretty soon. Micmac go too. Your father, he know!"

Then Silvernail, holding the wide eyes of the listening boy, was inspired to dilate on the secret nature of the wild geese; what they meant in the exact economy of the creatures; what they stood for upon the swept floors of the sky; how they fasted before rising to their great continental flights; how the old leading drake always knew the exact time to lift, according to the weather; how they crossed the Great Barren Lands in a single night. As if intoning a dark tragedy, the Micmac revealed the one weakness of the wild geese: corn, the white man's corn. If weather prevented the farmers' getting their corn in and the country was not too crowded with houses, the geese would settle and stay with the corn, forgetting their call to the south, forgetting even their dead. They would become heavy, logy, and waddling, a fallen estate.

"You not believe word—look at barnyard goose!" said John Silvernail.

Bucky started up from his thoughts, numb, congealed from the growing chill. It was 'way past dark and he had a mile and a half to go. Ma would have worked up half a bender already. His legs were like a pair of boards, hard to get going as he started for home.

2

$\mathcal{T}$WO WEEKS PASSED AND MID-OCTOBER CAME. A STILL and bittersweet melancholy lay over the pinewoods, but beneath that stillness was a tocsin of fierce unrest, for this was the mad time for most of the forest. The rutting time of the antlered tribes, courting and migration time of wildfowl; time of drumming on logs, of fierce battles in forest glades and erratic, aimless flights through the woods without regard for safety or direction. This was the month when a single old-man partridge would defy deer, bear, and even moose in the rashness of the courting fever. The wild cry of loons sounded from the lake and the spruce groves echoed to the booming of grouse. Even the pheasants, who were a collected folk ordinarily, were a bit giddy and not quite themselves during this period when the hunter's moon was waxing.

The wild-goose flock didn't pass on because of one fallen bird, but continued to linger. And the rains held on intermittently. A backwoods farmer coming in to town bewailed the fact that mud was hub-deep in his fields, that his corn was not in, that most of what the weather hadn't ruined had been eaten by the geese at night. This had a particular and private significance for Bucky Calloway.

These lake woods lay directly under one of the game birds' sky paths between Hudson's Bay and the Everglades. In small gaggles and mighty V's the geese went down every fall before the first snows and up again in March with the first thaws. Occasionally, but not every year, they stopped on the lake for a time, as in this particular fall. They couldn't be counted on to stop, but when they did, they stayed a fortnight at least, passing over the Calloway clearing night and morning from the lake.

On the last day the geese stayed, Bucky went alone back among the marshes, passing the site of the old Indian village, away up the lake shore where the wastelands ended, to the hundred acres of swamp and pine that Cam had always wanted to file on as a timber claim. His idea was to learn what the geese did all day and where they concealed themselves, but no sight or sound rewarded him. He found signs though, many webbed tracks in the mud, enough to prove that this was where the geese had their secret place, as Cam had guessed. His father loved it out here. Bucky had a certain dream about this place.

Early dusk was falling when he turned homeward, just as the geese came over on their way back to the lake, but he could still see clearly through the gray— one line of the great V trailing out longer than the other, the mighty gander stretched out ahead, then the second in command, then the point of the wedge. They seemed hurrying tonight and flying carelessly low, Bucky told himself tensely, as faint shots began to sound from the direction of the town. When his eyes came down to earth again, he saw that Bridie Mellott had stopped her father's horse and buggy on the muddy road close by.

"Always hanging around," Bucky thought.

Bridie had the Mellott mare in the shafts today—old Agatha, who could manipulate the back-country roads in mud where no truck or flivver could move a yard.

"C'mon an' get in, Bucky," Bridie called. "I'm going around by your place."

The boy kicked the heavy balls of mud from his boots and climbed up beside her. Bridie was a slim, freckled half boy, Bucky's age and almost as tall. Always there had been a bond between these two. Bridie and her pa held out against the town's ridicule of Cam Calloway and his brood. There were times when these two—Bridie in blue jeans like any boy—had had wonderful days together in the woods, hunting, fishing, even trapping. Bridie was almost as good as Bucky himself on the trail and at such times he could forget she was nothing but a girl. But there were other times, particularly of late—Bridie in dresses just hanging around and evincing a tiresome interest in Bucky's affairs—that made him wish he'd never known her. Getting sort of pretty, she was, too; pretty and silly.

Bridie was in jeans today, but working in the dresses phase.

"Bet I know where you've been," she said. "Out trying to find where the wild geese are nesting."

"Supposin' I have," Bucky said sullenly.

"What makes you care so, Bucky?"

He didn't answer.

"I mean, what makes you take 'em on like they're your special business?"

"The wild goose is my totem," Bucky said with heat. "I'm goin' to have one tattooed on my chest when I get money enough."

"Yes indeedy, and I expect you'll be goin' off with 'em sometime when they go, same as Cam does."

"Who told you that?"

"They all think you won't be long here."

"When the time comes I'll go an' not before. Let 'em laugh at me. I don't care. I got no use for them either. I'll—"

"They don't laugh at you when we're around," Bridie said.

"I could tell 'em all a lot about the geese, though, an' why they're staying on this fall an' why they don't always—"

"Tell me, Bucky."

"Might as well tell the whole town as tell you an' I ain't goin' to, not yet. You couldn't keep anything overnight."

"I could so!"

He was silent again for a space, then: "I've been thinking a lot. I'm goin' to do something in this world— I'm goin' to be somebody some day." He gestured around with a wide, vague sweep of his arm. "I'll do it. You wait an' see. I'll make the town laugh out of the other side of its face—"

"I know you will, Bucky."

The way she said it made him look at her squarely for a moment. He grew self-conscious then, as if ashamed of his outbreak.

"Pa wants to know is everything all right at your place, with Cam away and all," she said, after a bit.

Bucky nodded. "Shuh, we're makin' out."

They came in sight of the Calloway cabin, weathered gray among the pine trees overlooking the lake. Its clearing was like a scar among the trees. Not much in the way of a farm site; not much good for timber either; "pretty much nothing," as the townsfolk always said. Cam Calloway, more nimrod than yeoman, always clung to the trees. He had "taken up" this hundred-acre tract from old Doane Shattuck, the landman, two years before on small quarterly payments, but beyond building a split-log cabin, little had been done by way of improvement. But ostensibly he was a backwoods farmer. With Bucky's help he had cleared a meager two acres, had fought the stumps and stones, and each summer raised a patch of corn, potatoes, and some other garden truck. But all this was summer makeshift for Cam. Rangy and hound-lean, with a black Indian mane of hair, Cam was a true son of the wilderness; he was known to have a contempt for the orthodox ways of farmers. Life for him didn't really begin till fall set in and he could take up the activities of the trap line and hunting trail.

He knew the trackless region around the Swiftwater and the Kennebec like the palm of his hand. Winters he made a fair living along his trap lines. During the fall he picked up considerable money acting as a guide to hunters out after birds or deer, or sometimes even moose, fifty miles to the north. But never wild geese. Cam never shot at geese, nor would he allow anyone with him to shoot them. Once he lost a fifty-dollar guiding fee by fiercely knocking aside the gun barrel of a wealthy sportsman who was just aiming at a passing flock.

Bridie's prying eyes took in everything as they approached the Calloway clearing. Half a dozen chickens scratched in the dooryard. Old Scissorbill, the tame crow, was moving about in his wooden cage out back. Except for a single patch of corn that still stood, weeds had fired up all over the cleared ground.

"Looks like you've not turned over any ground for spring planting," Bridie said. "If you was aimin' to, Pa'd be proud to help."

11

"No call. We're like to be movin' anyway," Bucky gave out. "Lemme out here."

He climbed the fence and struck across the muddy field, glad to be rid of her. The gangling body was racing and winning, stoop-shouldered, against his overtaxed vitality.

Fifteen and a half, stoic and uncompromising, Bucky was more serious about life than any man. So much that was magnificent and maudlin, glorious and sentimental, to be lived up to at fifteen. The fires of idealism and glamour flamed in him fiercely.

Somehow Bucky knew Cam was home before he reached the clearing. As always a sort of bubble got going somewhere under his breastbone at the thought there was something that only Cam could give him, and he had been missing it for three whole weeks. He plunged forward headlong, then slowed to a walk again. He was eager, tearful, melting with affection, yet he was afraid. Always with Bucky there was the fear that Cam might go on and on like the geese and not return, and now his very breath hung at pause.

3 ~~~~~~~~~~~~~~~~

CAM STOOD BY THE DAUBED-CLAY FIREPLACE, HIS HEAD bent, his spare figure slumped and dejected. Hollows were under his eyes and in the dark planes of his face that were usually fulsome from the fires within.

He and Ma had been having it hot and heavy. Ma was sure puckered. Bucky knew by the attitude of Viney, his nine-year-old sister, and the intent quiet of old Sounder, the hound, who lay by the fire, in his brown eyes the look he had when he heard sounds he did not understand.

Bucky was glad he had not been there. Cam was whittled down to his smallest point again. That hurt. Cam looked ill and ravaged, but nothing was said about where he had been. Nothing would be, Bucky knew.

He just stood, embarrassed and delighted, filling his eyes with his father. Cam's quick dark glance caught and met the glow in Bucky's face. For the next hour the boy simply stood close or sat close. Cam scarcely spoke for a time, waiting for his wife's anger to spend its fuel. Lide Calloway was forty, made of the same general stuff as Cam, but more combustible. Part cata-mount, he always said of her, with a touch of pride. She had put up with much; their life had been a series of flights into new territory, always into the unsurveyed, away from the security that women want. But she was married irrevocably to the greater, deeper side of Cam. Little demonstration between them, but the depth of that tie was always to be felt. Part of Ma's rancor was always fear for Cam, the same fear that Bucky knew.

Presently there was a scratching sound at the kitchen wall. Cam opened a trap door and old Scissorbill came in from his wooden cage. He hopped onto Cam's shoulder and rasped "Haw" in a coarse, jeering way.

There was a wicked gleam in the bird's canny eye and a world of wile in the sly cant of its head. Old Sounder got up uneasily at the sight of him. He and all the barnyard creatures lived in fear of the crow's black scissor beak. But beneath the swashbuckling persona that masked Scissorbill's ways lay a strange depth of affection for humans.

Cam talked a bit as he fed the crow bits of food. Scissorbill sat hunched up in his rusty black raiment, looking like some corrupt old Prime Minister, or an undertaker of the old school. His watchful, hooded eyes seemed to have black night in their depths. Even Ma Calloway was chary of the creature.

"Heard somewheres that crows live to be old as humans," Cam said. "Wonder how old this 'un really is."

"Old enough to resign an' live on others anyway," Ma Calloway grumbled. "I'd hoped he'd fly off with some of his thievin' kind this fall, but not him. He's found him a good thing an' he's fixin' to stick by it."

"He sets a heap o' store by us."

"Sets a heap by our store o' food," Ma said acidly.

"We'd never get shut of him short of shootin' now," Cam said. "An' I couldn't do that."

A shadow passed the window and there was a thump at the door and a pitiful bawl. Keg, the tame bear cub Cam and Bucky had brought home that spring, after Cam had shot its mother, was begging to come in by the fire. But Ma Calloway opened the door and belabored its fat stern with a broom.

"Aw, Ma." Bucky's voice dripped misery. "Now he's cryin'!"

"Keg's a crybaby. Keg's a crybaby," echoed Viney gleefully.

The cub's eyes did seem actually wet with tears and he wriggled, whimpered, and hung his head with all the pitiful exaggeration of a spoiled child. Bucky got some scraps from a box where he kept food for the animals and he and Viney went outside to comfort Keg. They left him in his shed mumbling over a heel of bread.

"Critters, critters," Ma was complaining. "Fair clawin' holes in the door to get inside. Eatin' us back into the woods, they are. If they was only barnyard critters. But no. It's varmints of the woods we must fetch home an' care for now, an' us with hardly enough to pay our tax. It ain't right nor Christian. Even the Good Book says that birds may light on your head, but you needn't let 'em nest in your hair."

"They been a world o' fun for the young'uns," Cam defended. "An' somethin' by way o' learnin', too."

Ma went on ranting over the stove, but it was mere diminishing thunder now. Cam was back. Life had taken hold of the place again.

Supper was a poor affair. There was only a strip of side pork and a pan of cornmeal Ma had cooked.

Bucky was slipping into his place at table when Ma's voice cut at him from the stove: "You, Bucky, an' Viney too, go wash your dirty hands. An' don't be afeard to splash your faces a mite, too; it'll not hurt you."

15

Something crackled in Bucky's shirt as he bent to wash.

"Gosh, I near forgot. Picked up a lot of trashy mail in town. Mostly for Ma, I guess. Ol' Briscoe was about to burn it, he said."

"Burn it!" Ma fired up. "You tell Jim Briscoe to let be with my mail! Here, hand it over, you scaper."

Bucky gave her five open-ended envelopes, advertising circulars and such. He and Cam exchanged a long slow wink over Ma's shoulder. Nearly a year before, Cam had seen a personal ad in an old magazine which read: "Would you like to receive mail every day in the month? If so, send name and address and ten cents in coin." The ad had not lied. Cam's dime had been hard at work ever since in Ma Calloway's name. Never a week passed but brought her a batch of catalogues, or a sheaf of surefire bargains in everything from hairpins to caterpillar tractors. As Cam himself scarcely received a letter once a year, Ma's ego got a subtle workout. Rain, snow, or shine, Bucky and Viney were forever being sent in to the post office. It kept Ma in reading matter and helped dispel the sapping loneliness.

"You fellers draw up an' set to," she said, "while I just glance over this mail." Her tone was sharp and preoccupied. "Sowbelly an' mush is our portion here, with the woods full of pa'tridge an' deer meat for the taking. I eat any more of it an' I'll be rootin' and squealin' with the critters out back. Bucky did get us a couple pa'tridge a week ago though," she added. "'Fore he got to studyin' so on the geese an' their secret doin's."

Bucky's eyes met Cam's.

"Well, your meat worries are over now, Liddy," Cam said, falling to with a great show of gusto. "I an' Bucky are goin' out right tomorrow, to lay us in a mess of wild birds an' some venison, 'fore I get caught up with a guidin' trip. We'll take the heavy rifle along with

the old ten-gage this time. High time Bucky was learnin'
to use the thirty-thirty as handy as he does the shotgun."

Bucky quivered with repressed excitement. Ma
sniffed:

"Yes, so's he'll be out in the woods all the time, 'stead
of only part, I s'pose. Happen you'd learn him to be
handy with the hoe as he is with the shotgun, we might
ketch up with taxes an' maybe buy us a stick or two of
new furniture. My sakes." She wet a thumb and turned
another page of her circular. "Beats all what a sight of
fine furniture a body can get for only eighty-nine
fifty. Enough to fill a two-three room house, it says
here, an' six drape-length curtains throwed in."

Cam snorted.

"Spindly stuff that'd break up like scantlin's would a
healthy man lean on it. Always hanker for whatever's
few an' fur an' hard to git," he said. "Back in the city now,
there's tomfools readin' fancy catalogues about solid
handmade tables an' chairs burnt an' polished such as
these here. Ain't a city hunter comes out here but tries
to bribe 'em off o' me. An' these deer-foot door handles
an' the panther skins on the floor—they'd fair pawn off
wife or child for a set o' them for their huntin' lodges an'
the like. But out here we got to hanker for them match-
wood things the city's sick of." Cam had made all his
own furniture, fine pieces of hand-tooled pine and cedar,
during those midwinter days when blizzards snowed
the family in for a week at a time. He was handy with
tools, had even done a little carving on the side. The
cabin floors were covered with the soft skins of deer,
bear, and panther—carefully scraped, beaten, and softened by Cam.

"All the same, I'd admire someday to set me down in
a house with real curtains, snap-on lights, and reg'lar
rugs to the foot," Ma said. "Maybe when I go in to get
my sinuses trepined I'll get a taste of such." For five

years Ma had suffered violent periodic pains in the head which only a city specialist could ever cure, Doc Waters said.

"Speakin' of guidin' trips, who-all you expect to come out this year?"

"Mr. Corey, of course," Cam said. "An' old Cash Wyble, cuss him, an' too many more of his stripe."

"Let's hope Doane Shattuck an' his brother come out for a long trip this fall," Ma said dourly. "A fine moose head an' a pretty week up in the woods might help our case a mite. Somethin's got to be done there right quick."

Cam's face darkened. The ever-present problem of overdue payments on his hundred timbered acres had been as inescapable as his own shadow for a year past. But Cam had his pride.

"Shattuck's got him a watch-chain belly now," he said scornfully. "Seen him not so long back in his shiny car. Don't do no walkin' now. Why his tongue'd be hangin' out of his mouth a foot should he follow a trail a couple hours." Cam, though well past forty, was still lean-flanked as his hound, and could follow the dog all day and part of the night. "Don't know as I'd guide the old shoat should he show up," Cam added. "There's some things you got to draw a halt on in respect to the varmints themselves, I'll declare. But I mistrust we'll not be needin' ary of Doane Shattuck's favors soon. I been doin' some cold-out studyin' on plans for this comin' winter."

Cam paused an artful minute to tamp tobacco in his pipe bowl. Bucky passed him a blazing pine splinter.

"Bucky here has got some size to him now," Cam went on. "Knows the woods an' the ways o' the varmints 's well as I. So I figger we should lay us in some extra traps an' let Bucky tend a line of his own."

A thrill ran along Bucky's spine. He gasped: "Tell me quick, Pa, you ain't spinnin' a lie-tale?"

"Nary tale," Cam said.

Viney was all eyes. Ma had laid aside her mail.

"Bucky ain't a tad no longer an' that's a fact," she said. "Speakin' o' size that is, an' appetite! But let it be hoein' or chores round the place an' he's puny an' pulin' again, or hard to catch as a new bird dog. But I'm fearsome of seein' him spend his whole time in the woods, goin' wild an' hairy an' low-down, like some we know in these parts. We'd had plans for educatin' the boy."

"An' still have," Cam said. "But last year he learnt all's to be learnt at Swiftwater Grade School. To send him to town school's goin' to take money an' there's no quicker way o' makin' it than furs. They'll might' nigh swap for gold this year. No, Bucky'll do best with what I can make out to learn him, for a spell."

Ma was silenced. Cam went on, authority in his tone now, for he spoke of his own realm.

"Cold winter, goin' to be," Cam pronounced. "I take note, comin' up through Tamarack, the buck rabbits already whiter'n Sol Wire's mule. Fur'll soon be prime. Now I figger on lettin' Bucky run the old line 'round the lake shore this winter, whiles I lay me out a new line up north along the Little Jackpine. I'll swear, it looks mighty promisin' there. I been a heap hindsighted or I'd of branched out up thataway afore this.

"Now them traps—I already ordered 'em from Stemline's store. Aye cod, with the two of us workin' separate lines thataway, I figger we can just about take double catch for the season. By spring we'd stand to be rich as doe's cream. We can maybe work in that little trip o' yours to the sinus shark, Liddy!"

They would lay out both trap lines together, he said, so that each would know the location of every trap. Now and then they could change off and cover each other's territory. There'd be nothing to it all, up until the snow got deep, Cam said. Then they'd have to use snowshoes.

It would take two days then to cover their lines and round back home again and that would mean each man would have to spend the night in a snow camp at the end of his line.

"Each man." Bucky felt the hair stir on his nape, the way Pa said that. He grew more stolid, he had to hold so hard against the rising flood of feeling.

"Think you'll be ascairt to sleep alone in the deep woods, son?" Cam asked. "It's right fearsome at first."

"Not me." Bucky's tone discounted all concern. "Anyhow I'd have an ax an' a rifle an' plenty grub and blankets," he said.

Cam chuckled. "We'd be sleepin' out about once every week in bad weather. We'll have to build us reg'lar log caches for the extra traps an' grub an' such —big enough to sleep a man. A dog too, on occasion," he added slyly. "But before ary thing is done by way of trappin' we got us a sight of huntin' to do. Got to lay us in plenty wild birds an' rabbits an' a sight of jerked deer meat against winter weather. Rain's over for the year. It's comin' a spell of clear cold or I miss my guess. Geese'll be leavin' the lake tonight."

"Now no, Pa!" Bucky cried. "Only today I found it— what we been lookin' for long gone. Back in the marshes it is. I was fixin' to show you in the morning."

"Too bad, son. But migration's a thing'll not wait on the likes of us. It's timed an' certain-sure as the risin' an' settin' of the sun ball. But you can show me the place all the same. They eaten ary o' the corn we left 'em?"

Bucky shook his head.

"When'll we get started, tomorrow, Pa?"

"By gray streaks we should be on our way," Cam said. "Fetch out the two guns, Bucky. We'd best look to 'em now."

"Let be on all your hustle," Ma Calloway clipped.

"Neither of you chaps is escapin' to the woods 'fore you get me in plenty wood an' water an' help cut up for the sausage."

"We'll leave all shipshape 'fore we go," Cam promised. He squinted down a gun barrel and muttered. "There's just not the light here for sightin' rust," he said. "Happen you could fetch out the Radiant Beam for a bit, Liddy, so we could see what's toward?"

Ma rose with a fine mixture of reluctance and eagerness. Cam followed her with a beam in his eye as she went to get her new lamp from its box in the kitchen. It was a blue-glass affair with a special circular wick and its white china shade was strung with dangling crystals. This was Ma's prime treasure and she brought it out only for special company and holidays, lest dogs or children break it.

Murmurs accompanied Cam's gratified sigh as he held each gun barrel to the new bright light. "Bright's a bugle," he pronounced. "Even the old twenty-two. See you been over 'em recent, Bucky."

"I looked at 'em a week back." Bucky was noncommittal.

"We'm mobilized proper," Cam chuckled.

In the silence that followed a faint, far *ya-honk* jerked Bucky to his feet. It came from high sky. He flung open the cabin door. From far up in the misty blackness, directly overhead, other, fainter sounds dropped earthward, wild, subdued ecstasy of passage. The easy honk of the old leading gander rippled in repetition along his formation lines like the clink of each link in a shaken chain.

"They're circlin'," Cam's voice came quietly. "They'll like to quarter once, then steady away an' head south. For Florida an' Mexico, where all the wealthy are headin' now. We'll not see 'em again till April. Aye gonnies, what a life." He sighed.

They listened till the deep pipe of the gander boomed again, farther away, then the wild high cadence diminished till the sounds came faint as the chink of falling coins and were gone.

Cam sat gazing pensively into the fire. In Bucky's chest was a feel like funeralizing. He still felt the gooseflesh on his skin, the way his father had named the night of passage. Cam was always right on these matters of the woods. Bucky knew how he got game; how he would sit in a forest clearing still as stone until the wild things drifted up and carried on their life within a dozen yards of the small, neutral figure.

"You sure can figger just what the critters'll do, Pa," he said. "How come you always know so well?"

"I've had a mort o' years to learn it in, son. Been in the woods since I was tad-high to a toadstool. All a man's got that critters ain't is the sense to outfigger 'em. He's a pretty sorry somethin' after forty years if he can't outsmart 'em an' guess 'em down." Cam stretched his arms high above his head and groaned: "Aye cod, I'm wore out. I could do with bed."

"Me too," Bucky said.

He climbed the thin, spike-worn ladder to his bed in the quarter loft under the eaves. Cam made ready to turn in in the wide bunk he and Ma occupied in the corner of the cabin. Ma sighed.

"I'll just set a short spell an' finish with this mail," she said importantly and drew up under the new lamp.

PROPERTY OF
FRANKFORT SCHUYLER CENTRAL
HIGH SCHOOL LIBRARY
FRANKFORT, NEW YORK 13340

4

CAM WAS RIGHT ABOUT THE WEATHER, TOO. THE CLOUD-less sky next morning was like hard green enamel. There was no breeze and the stillness of a prayer lived beneath the high conifers around the Calloway clearing. From down by the lake came the faintest elfin tinkle of shell ice formed during the night chill. The ventriloquial call of a pair of loons out on the darkening waters struck a note as melancholy as the remote line of pine spires against the eastern sky.

"The crazy folk are right chipper this mornin'," Cam said, referring to the loons. "Geese gone. Always sets 'em up a mite, havin' the lake to themselves."

Cam was chopping the fixings for Ma's sausage, while Bucky piled seasoned pine wood by the cabin door.

"What makes 'em call so skeery an' addled?" he asked.

"All that's laid out in a tale the Micmacs tell," Cam said.

"Tell it, Pa," Viney begged.

"Well, in times long gone there was a beauteous Indian girl in the tribe named Leaf Down, she was

23

that dainty an' delicate. She was in love with a young brave, name of Eagle Seizer, an' they'm soon to become man an' wife when a medicine man from a neighborin' tribe is fair took over by Leaf Down's beauty. He's old enough to've fathered the pair of 'em an' should a-knowed better, but he goes a grain crazy at sight of the girl. He's a powerful high shaman, right handy at black art an' such, an' he casts a spell over the lovers. It does him nary good though; their love is too strong. But finally he gets Leaf Down's pa in his power an' makes him give over the girl in marriage.

"Eagle Seizer comes back from his huntin' an' the minute he hears of this he lights a rag out for the shaman's village, with his war ax an' his bow an' arrows, but the shaman's men are watching for him. They waylay him an' kill him an' throw his body into the lake. Leaf Down carries on scandalous when she hears of this an' the first chance she gets she goes down to the lake an' throws herself in from a high rock. Now up to that time the loon was a stone-dumb critter, the Micmacs say, but the spirits of them two lovers entered the birds, an' from that day on you could hear 'em grievin' crazylike over the wrong that was done 'em. From that day on no Micmac has ever killed a loon an' they're everly bran-fired mad at ary white man that'll do such."

"I'd not," Viney said with heat. "Even if one come a-trailin' a wing up to my house, I'd think of the other a-mowerin' out there an' I'd get it back to water."

"You'd best get back to your own water an' the dishes," Ma Calloway called from the kitchen. "This is Saturday an' I'm bound to have your help to redd up the house."

Cam and Bucky got free of Ma about an hour after breakfast and struck out along the lake shore. The air was like golden wine. On the hardwood rises behind the cabin the frost fires were in full blaze. The hard maples glowed rose-red and in the thickets beneath, the antlers of the staghorn sumac held sprays of deep blood red and old gold. Here and there a towering white ash rose like a royal plume of purple. Down close to the ground ran streaks of dull garnet and bright buttercup yellow where the sassafras was turning. The squat spicebush had turned to gamboge yellow.

But richest of all in pigment were the occasional red oaks on the high ridges. They made the woods seem on fire. Even Cam had to pause in wonder at a small island of these rising above a shimmering lake of yellow beeches.

The heaped leaves rustled underfoot. Then the silent stretches of pine and spruce began. Here there were vaults of blue-black welted shadow, jungles and labyrinths of windfalls and down timber, and many ancient logs, the perfect drumming and courting places for partridge.

As always, Cam was a different being in the woods. Days like this he became a boy again. He never took a dog on such hunts. Stalking and still-hunting were his way, and, besides, he detested rousing the countryside with the baying of hounds.

Bucky was high-fire, more alive than he had been for months. As they tramped, he told Cam what he had found out about the geese back in the marshes, and about his fight with Whit Turner. He had had to tell Ma the first night because of his bruises, but he'd wanted to wait and tell Cam when they were alone.

"You done right to foller your feelin's thataway," Cam said. "A chap's got to have the courage of his conversation, all times, an' all our line's always stuck up for the geese. Town thinks we're addled, root an' branch, so I've heard it told. But all that don't differ none to us. You'd best get fixed for more trouble one day soon though,

Bucky. 'Twould be a heap diff'rent—him bringin' the fight to you."

"I can take care of myself," Bucky said. "I'm sorry I did it now. Must o' gone a mite daft, seein' that goose drop. I don't hone to feud with anybody."

"I know you don't, son, an' I'm right glad of it."

A startled *quit, quit* sound from the thickets a hundred yards ahead; then a muffled whir of wings. A covey of partridge roared across an open glade. Cam's gun leapt to his shoulder like light itself and clapping echoes fled away among the hills. A speckled bird peeled off from the flock and plummeted downward in the brush.

Bucky had been a breath too slow to aim and had held fire, following the inbred code of the region never to waste a shell, always to make a single shot do. From long practice father and son had developed a teamwork. They were like separate parts of the same machine. Their gun barrels followed automatically each flurry of birds. In the split second in which the partridge rocketed from sight, the decision was made as to who would shoot. A single word from the first to draw bead and the other held fire, unless it was a covey of more than half a dozen; then both would fire simultaneously.

They set off inland from the lake, moving single file, Cam in the lead. They moved with remarkable silence, for each had the still-hunter's privy foot and the rare woods-traveling mind. Hurry was forgotten. Cam was a millionaire where time was concerned.

From high sky and from every glen came the rousing tocsin of the game bird's courting and mating calls. Killdeer sounded their irascible warning, which sounded like "Keep away, keep away."

In the next mile they brought down five more partridge. Then they entered a stretch of hardwoods with willow thickets running down to the stream banks. Here long lines of rabbits slipped silently away to all sides before them, each line led by a big old buck. Already snow-white in their winter coats, they could be seen for a hundred yards amid the winter brush. Even in their secret forms, they stood out now like nubbins of unmelted snow against the dry stems and dark brown earth.

They shot eight bucks before they quit the willow strip. Their meat was already firm and prime.

"Aye cod, them poor foolish dobbers," Cam said. "They figger they'm safe in their hidey holes, same as in spring an' summer when all the leaves is helpin' 'em. They'm pure fooled by nature an' the season. I declare, it's cold-out murder, shootin' 'em. We'm a fair load o' meat now. We'd best take 'em up on the ridge yonder an' clean 'em after we eaten a bite. Rid ourselves of twenty-five-pound weight."

They sat down with their backs to an ancient beech and ate the bacon sandwiches and wedges of cornbread Ma had made up. Afterward they lay on their backs looking up between the leafless branches. Bucky was lonely-happy, with that bittersweet joy he knew only when he and Cam were alone. He stretched, sighed, and groaned.

"Pity it can't be like this every day o' the world, Pa."

"It's a God's mercy it ain't, son," Cam chuckled. "Else there'd be nothing to set it off from the rest an' all would go stale, like beer with the cap off. The best part of ary thing, even love, is the plannin' an' lookin' toward it in the sorry times."

The southern migration was reaching its final height in these last days before snow flew. A few gaggles of wild geese still went over, flying high, with no thought of stopping short of the Great Lakes. Lower down, duck of many kinds went hurtling down the sky. Only a thousand feet above the forest occasional bands of scaup came down the wind in dark streamers. Families of blue-winged teal shot past wedges of slower-flying ducks.

Once, as they watched, a company of canvasbacks came down the sky in a whizzing parallelogram, their long red heads and necks outstretched—grunting as they flew. These speed kings of the ducks moved at a hundred and thirty miles an hour.

"What's them gray-black specks 'way up there with the sun ball glintin' on 'em?" Bucky said, pointing. "I took 'em for a cloud tatter first, but I make out their wings. There's two long strings of 'em."

"Them'll be widgeon an' tern, son. I can't rightly make 'em out, but I know by their speed. They come from clear up on the Artic Sea. They got no truck for such as us an' our puny lake. They'll make no stop, 'cept maybe once on the big lakes, till they get to Mexico an' beyond. They'm the long-distance fliers o' the lot. The tern hold the cold-out record for far flyin' o' the whole mort o' winged critters. They start out from the Artic Sea an' fly an' fly like they was addled, never stoppin' till they come to the South Pole Sea each year. They nest as far north an' as far south as they can find a morsel o' land. Takes 'em nigh six months goin' down an' six months comin' back, so even their courtin' an' matin' has to be done along the way. They be a fair match to you, I reckon, for traipsin' their days away an' wantin' to see all creation. Now see kin you tell me which is the speediest o' all the flyin' things."

"I'd name the ol' canvasback first," Bucky said.

"You'm wrong. It's the little ol' bat-bird that your ma's so 'feared of when its circlin' round of a summer night. A critter that ain't even a pure bird, but a pindlin' mouse-varmint with wings onto it. But in straightaway flyin' it'll leave ary bird behind like it was stuck in a bog-hole. It'll do better'n two hundred mile an' hour, so the books say."

Cam lit his pipe and began slitting the bellies of the rabbits open. Bucky followed suit. As they worked the

trees became peopled with a company of rusty black-
birds, who sang together like a regiment of creaking
wheelbarrows as they cocked rakish heads to spy on
the men below.

"Them black rascals is due to get snow-bogged in a
norther for their cur'ous ways," Cam said. "Many's the
time I come onto a round score of 'em froze bone-solid
under a tree where a chill snap catched 'em. They'm
built a lot like a flighty woman, everly dawdlin' an' gos-
sipy an' pryin' into another's business. A straightaway
mile or two'd be a long flight for 'em, I mistrust, with so
much in the world to see an' talk about. They'd ought to
be far down in York State by now."

When the rabbits were cleaned they strung them together by their hind-leg tendons, the partridge with
them.

"We'll hang 'em all on a high bough an' get 'em as we
come back," Cam said.

As he got to his feet he uttered a low groan and stood
rubbing his hips and thighs with his two hands.

"Ain't the man I was," he muttered wryly. "Take me a
week or two to curry the kinks out an' get back in shape,
I reckon."

For a space his gaze was lost in the distant woods, a
grayish look on his face.

5 ~~~~~~~~~~~~~~~~~~~~~

$\mathcal{I}$LLNESS AND PHYSICAL WEAKNESS WERE ALMOST UN-
known in the Calloway household. A shadow fell over
Bucky at Cam's words and the gray look that crossed his
father's face, but he said nothing. Each took up his gun
and for a time thereafter they gave over all talk and
tramped silently, using their eyes and ears and every
sense to analyze the new range they were entering.

The Little Jackpine Valley was one of those remote
places, which still exist in the Northern wilds, where the
wilderness in all its olden meanings had held out from
the beginning against the inroads of man. Few hunters
ever went there; even the Indians rarely visited the place.
The valley had never been trapped in Cam's memory.
Even he had never been to the valley's head, far up on
old Sugarloaf Mountain.

The lower half of the valley was a jackpine forest,
where the trees on the slopes grew thick as a crop of
devilgrass. Farther up toward Sugarloaf, the pines gave
way to spruce and the valley pitched downward in a
series of rocky ramps. Down these, from somewhere in
the mountain's heart, a small stream a rod and a half

wide came rushing and plunging in many a miniature fall and boiling cataract—the Little Jackpine, which even in winter did not freeze along its headwaters.

Both Cam and Bucky could read the silent speech of places, and what the valley said seemed vaguely antagonistic. Animal signs were all different here; there were few birds and only occasional deer signs and the rabbits were wary. Twice they sighted a red fox.

The valley's length lay open, like a slot in the mountainside, to the fury of the northwest storms, and the stream bed had become choked with almost inaccessible jungles of down logs, brush, and windfalls. These weather-bleached masses of branches formed nightmare tangles that seemed caught in a permanent hysteria.

Cam cut careful trails around these, leaving blazes for future guidance. From the midst of these tangles tiny snow-white ermine reared to eye them cautiously.

"Fur sign better'n I seen in a scad o' years," Cam said. "There's a mint o' bounty in here for the takin', son. We'll start layin' our line out come first snow."

They pressed on through brush ever more wild and forbidding as the pine gave way to spruce and the stream hissed and leaped among its rocks. Camp birds fluttered up from bare bushes. Squirrels chattered, with crisp, ratchety calls.

Cam paused, pointing to a grouse that had been killed, the skeleton left intact.

"Hawk," he said. "Wolf or lynx would have ate all an' cracked the bones. Mink would have tore the breast open."

A bit farther on the great splayed tracks of a lone moose came down to the stream bank and crossed the valley. The two stood looking at the trail. Cam's black eyes gleamed. A tingle went through Bucky at the size of the tracks.

"Them tracks is big enough for old Lophorn hisself, I do declare," Cam said.

Old Lophorn was known to every hunter. He was an anachronism, apparently the last of his kind left in that section, so named for the peculiar palmation of his left antler. A big bull of mature years, he was so woods-wise that he had survived season after season, in spite of the efforts of numerous hunters to bring him low. But there were not a few woodsmen in the country who were proud of the tall bull and saw in his exceptional size and prowess a promise for better hunting in years to come. Some of these, including Cam himself, had refrained from putting a ball into Lophorn when he came in fair range.

The sheer joy of the trail had taken Bucky over now, and he was lonely-happy again. The weight of his light pack, the heft of his gun, were part of it.

Once they sighted a mink in prime winter coat. An otter with snaky neck arched in curiosity, paused fearlessly before lancing into the water.

"Not even a grain fearsome," Cam marveled. "Could 'a picked him off with the light gun. Oh it's a virgin range we come onto, Bucky."

"I disremember ever seein' such a mort o' critters, bird or varmint, as this year," Bucky said. "It's like they was all askin' to be kilt dead an' done with. What makes huntin' that way one year an' another so pindlin' an' scanty?"

"You'm hit on one o' the prime secrets o' nature there, son," Cam said. "We'm now in a ninth year o' fatness an' plenty. Nine years all the critters has been breedin' an' buildin' up to a peak o' plenty, till they'm a rabbit growin' on every bush. But then along comes the tenth year, the lean time—'The Year o' No Rabbits,' the Indians always call it. It's like nature'd turned pure sick o' their wastrelin' ways an' every tenth year set out to weed 'em down to root again. I reckon if'n she didn't take a hand like that, times, they'd breed like Talt Bingham an' his woman done on Hat Creek, with their seventeen married children. Breedin' an' begettin' till hell won't have it no more an' but for a higher hand humans themselves'd not find room left in the land. But nature she brings sickness an' a mort o' mishaps, an' plague worse than was writ in the Book, cuttin' down all tribes till they'm on the rag edge o' 'bliteration an' there's naught but a small handful left to carry on the line. Next year we'm due to see that, Bucky. We can hunt through that willow slash back yonder an' we'll find but a rabbit or two left an' them rickety an' ailin'. Every ten year, reg'lar as clock tick, the lean time comes. 'Twas a Micmac hunter first told me of that, 'way back when I was only tad-size. The Indians knowed about it from times long gone an' always prepared for it beforehand. In all my time in the woods I never seen it fail. So we got to make fur harvest this year, Bucky. Next winter it'll be scarce worth the work of layin' our traps."

Bucky was silent. Minutes later he asked, after long mulling:

"Ain't there a critter in all the Lord's lot that nature ain't got it in for?"

"I was waitin' for you to ax that," Cam said. "They'm a small few. There's the wild goose for one, an' the quail. The reason there's that both has strict breedin' laws o' their own, laws a sight better'n most humans know. An' the deer ain't hardly affected by the die-off year neither. It's the rifle an' the cougar that thins out the deer folk."

Presently as they climbed up out of a gloomy ravine, an ancient, half-dead pine called their attention by its great size. It was a couple of centuries old and evidently the only remnant of its day left in the valley. Round about, rotting stumps showed how some long-ago fire had demolished its fellows in bygone days, long before the white man's coming. The bark was falling away in patches. Half the boughs were bare and dead. A great hollow at its base showed the inroad many a fire had made into its heart.

Cam knelt and peered up into the dark hollow bole.

"We'll plant us a trap or two in that hollow, come first snow, Pa," Bucky said.

Cam shook his head.

"Bear tree," he said. "Best let it be. Take a look at it again, come January. I mistrust we'll come onto a roomer here." He moved round the tree. "Look there, Bucky." He pointed. "That there's the blaze mark o' the last bear that slept here. A male bear'll always leave his mark, happen he finds a thing or a spot that purely suits his fancy. Many's the time I've seed one carvin' his 'nitials like on a tree. He'll stand up with his back again' the trunk, a-naggin' an' a-mumblin' an' measurin' his length. Then he'll turn round an' reach high as he can to claw his sign for all comers to read. It's a cold-out location blank like a man'll put up on a gold strike, givin' his size an' smell an' the state of his spunk, an' it's only a bear with a whole lot longer reach that'd think o' tanglin' with him over his claim."

From high up in the tree a squirrel began scolding. He was a big gray and the volume of his voice was deepened by the resonant hollow wood of the tree till it filled all the surrounding woods.

"Take the light gun an' see can you bark that feller," Cam said. "'Twill take close shootin', he's a good hundred an' twenty foot up."

Bucky waited a full minute till the squirrel had run out along the side of a limb, then fired. A white chip jumped from beneath the big gray and he was flung into the air to fall earthward.

"Thunder an' gimpsum!" Cam exclaimed. "That were as pretty a barkin' shot as ever I seen. I ain't even goin'

34

to compete again' that, son, 'cause it couldn't be bettered. It's perfect." He indulged in one of his almost soundless laughs. "You been doin' a sight o' practicin', I'll declare. Last year you had me fair tied at all tests. Now on I'll be put to it to hold my own. You grow a mite more an' you'll have me shaded there, too."

A half hour later they turned homeward. They had found what they had hoped for, and something else besides. It was just beginning to look late. It was strange walking in the shadows of the valley bottom. Streamers of wind-blown snow streaked out from Sugarloaf Peak and the sun made them burn like wild torches. A chill breeze came sucking down from the heights, whispering eerily of snow. A dozen times as they went down-trail Cam stopped abruptly to look behind him and to all sides. Bucky would stop in the same instant.

"Queer," Cam muttered. "A full hour past, I had a right smart feelin' we're bein' watched an' follered. I still got it."

"I had it too, Pa. It's mighty fearsome back yonder, ain't it?"

"It ain't a bear." Cam evaded the question. "Maybe some young fool of a lynx cat, figgerin' he'd like to play with us. A lynx is a tomfool for follerin' humans, but mostly you'm able to catch him at it."

They watched and listened, and once Cam hurried back to the top of a rocky rise they had just quitted, but he saw nothing. He looked tired again and Bucky felt another worry pang.

They hastened now along the stream bank, not talking. The breeze sounded its ancient dirge in the treetops. The hiss of the stream made a hush that was more intense than clear silence. A muffled pocket of stillness.

Bucky chunked a stone into the boiling waters to show his unconcern, but it didn't do much good. There was something listening behind each tree and rock as they passed. It wouldn't stop a fellow and maybe it wouldn't harm him, directly. But it didn't like outsiders, Bucky felt. And the coming winter and all the olden meanings of this valley were its allies.

6

$\mathcal{T}$ODAY YOU FELLERS HAS GOT TO CHINK-STOP THESE windows with rags or summat, 'fore you high-tail it to the woods again," announced Ma Calloway at breakfast next morning. "I declare, with the north wind sucking in all the cracks, the drafts have fair takened over the place and every corner in it. A few more days and I'd catch my death an' the sinus too, soul alone here, and with no time for such fixin's."

"I pure forgot them windows," Cam said ruefully. "And it apt to come full winter any day now. Fetch in that old felt from the shed house, Bucky, an' we'll batten things proper. Then maybe if we bank the foundation with earth an' manure, your ma'll roast us a bird or two for an early noon bite, 'fore we leave," he added mildly.

"I could eat two whole pa'tridge myself," Bucky said, "an' a dozen taters an' half a pie."

"Your talk's bigger'n your bite, like always," Ma said. "But if you're feelin' that way you can pluck me four-five birds, 'fore you start to work."

"Yes, we'm meat a-plenty now," said Cam.

Ma turned on him. "Meat now, but what about later?

S'pose we might's well make it a picnic, now we got it, even if we take our belts in come midwinter."

Ma acted put upon, but Bucky knew she was happy.

"We'm aimin' to skip all leanness this year," Cam said. "Bucky an' I has found us a mint mine o' fur range up on the Little Jackpine."

"It's the skeeriest, wildest place you ever seen, Ma," Bucky said, "an' the varmints ain't even afeard of men."

"I disremember ever seein' better fur sign," Cam said. "With even a grain o' luck we'm due to be buyin' any an' all our fancy thinks of an' trustin' some o' our money to the bank, come spring."

"My fancy outrun my intelleck five years gone now," Ma sniffed. "But a body can always hope. By tomorrow," she went on, "one or both of you's got to go to town for the mail an' more vittles. I'm purely out o' flour now, an' sugar an' 'lasses an' sal'ratus. An' it's high time we had some real coffee in the house again. That store tea is a water-sprinkled thing, come winter, an' cocoa nor chic'ry was never meant for ary human to drink."

"I'll bribe Nat Stemline out o' a fair bill o' goods," Cam promised. "I'll tell him all about them fur signs too."

"Our bill don't run too much now," Ma said. "We went real lean through the fall. But even the Good Book says man can't live by bread alone. Nor neither can he by 'lasses an' meal, only just so long."

"We'll get you all the trimmin's," Cam promised. "The meat an' taters we got. Let's eat hearty, 'cause five days away an' we'll have deer meat to lay by. Figger we may as well have the chickens for table an' I may cure the two pigs, too, 'stead o' tryin' to carry 'em through the winter. We'll have our hands full with the traps."

"Some jerked venison an' a shoulder or two o' pork

in the smokehouse an' things'll look natural again. Pity is you can't cure that worthless bear cub, too."

"Now Ma, no!" wailed Viney and Bucky in unison.

"That do-less, no-count bear has et us out o' a pure carload o' food scraps through the spring an' summer, an' us contrivin' at best o' times. Furthermore, Cameron Calloway, he ain't a cub no more. He weighs more'n a man, a low-standing keg of a man, all cut down to belly an' appetite. An' not forgettin' deviltry. I'm afeard at times to go into my own yard when he's in a mind for huggin' an' wrasslin'."

"I'd bet on you, Ma, come to a tussle," Bucky laughed.

"You'd think he'd learn to look out for himself by now, but we'm babied an' mollied him to ditheration. How long's a body to put up with it?"

"I figgered he'd be long gone to the woods by now, or I'd put a foot down at the start," Cam said. "Figgered he'd nat'rally hibernate, come cold weather, but he don't show a sign. Looks like nothin' but the matin' call'll take him back to his kind. Poor little dobber, figgers he was borned here, most like, an' we'm his parents. Now we'm addled up his life for him with tame ways we'm purely responsible for him, looks like."

"Meanwhile he'm apt to go clean wild an' kill some of us in our beds."

Bucky ran into the yard where Keg was mumbling over an old bone. Viney followed.

"Watch us, Ma. Keg ain't even a mite fearsome, even when he's wrasslin'. He knows a sight o' tricks, too. Lookit!"

Bucky thrust an absurd dunce cap of paper on the cub's head and gave an order. Keg rose obediently on his hind legs and walked staggeringly round and round. His head was tilted ludicrously sidewise, his forepaws waved beseechingly in the air. Keg enjoyed the trick even more than the youngsters themselves.

Tiring of the game at last, Keg dropped and grappled lovingly with Bucky in a sort of football tackle, diligently searching his pockets for reward. Old Sounder rushed loyally in to join the scrimmage and Keg turned to engage him in a special sham battle. They rolled on the ground, bawling and barking blissfully.

Ever since he had been able to walk Keg had eaten and slept among the animals of the barnyard; he had played, fought and wrestled, learned to come when called, and taken chastisement on occasion, the same as the dog and the children, profiting by it all, particularly on the occasion which had earned him his name.

The Calloways had returned home one day to find their pet bawling in the clearing, with his head stuck fast in a small honey keg. Thereafter the name Keg remained as a fixture and it fitted the youngster as well as his own hide.

Cam stood watching and filling his pipe.

"How'm he to know he's ary different from the young-'uns, the dog, or the pig?" he said. "I mistrust nothin', not even a mirror-glass'd show him—short of the matin' call. We'm raised him to be a Calloway, Liddy, an' somehow we got to tide him through to another summer."

For the next two hours work took over the family. Cam and Bucky weatherproofed every crack and banked up the foundation against coming snow. At the end of that time Ma called everyone for the noon meal.

In the past twenty-four hours, leanness had fled before plenty and the Calloways foregathered each with a whole browned partridge on his plate. They fell to in silence.

Ma had no equal in the region in the preparation of wild game. She roasted her partridge slowly in two big Dutch ovens, tucking strips of bacon under the breast skin and stuffing the birds with onion and the tender, long-grained wild rice which Cam and Bucky garnered each summer from the marshland at the head of the lake. To Bucky, at least, partridge was the feast of all feasts.

"Grabbies!" Cam sighed at last. "They'm tender as snail horns, Liddy. Even these little bones, brown an' crisp like toast to the teeth. Oh there's no time o' the world like fall!"

Bucky was too busy with his plateful to speak. Even Viney had laid aside her new, ladylike ways to eat with her fingers. Cam spoke over his pipe when the meal was finished.

"Bucky an' I'll make that little trip to town this afternoon. We can get us another mess o' birds along the way. We got to have more shells an' see about them new traps."

"Reminds me, I got an important letter for you to mail," Ma said, going to the cupboard above the stove. "Put a stamp onto this an' drop another one inside. It's for their big double-size winter catalogue. I guess likely it'll be owllight 'fore you fellers get back."

"Don't expect us till you see us," Cam said. "We might stop by Alf Simes' place, or Jeth Mellott's."

Bucky gave an exaggerated groan.

"I purely hope Bridie won't be hangin' around there," he said.

"Bridie's sweet on Bucky, an' Bucky's sweet on her!" chanted Viney, giggling.

Bucky's face went dull-red with vexation.

"You don't know a bee from a bull's foot," he cried. "That's just a lie-tale they made up at school."

"I take note Bridie don't haunt this place like she used to," Ma remarked.

"She can't trail me round the woods no more," Bucky

said sullenly. "She'd make a feller the laugh-stock o' the town."

When he and Cam had been out on the trail a few minutes, Cam remarked casually: "What's this about you an' Bridie, son? Used to be you two was close as a pair o' wings, like. Always huntin' an' proggin' the woods together."

Bucky kicked at a big pine cone.

"I don't know. Used to be Bridie was good as any man," he said. "Knowed the woods an' critters good as I or you, almost. She'd hunt an' track all day. Then she turned uppity on me. Says she got no time for huntin'. Turned rabbity, too. Last summer, that was. Acted up like a pure fool, last time I stopped by her place. Had a ruffledy dress on an' was makin' herself a new face in front of me, with powder an' truck."

Cam shook with silent mirth.

"A girl-chap'll always turn finickin' after just so long," he said. "But all that's as the Lord intended, Bucky. Bridie's about turned fifteen now; time to show her feathers an' trail her wing a bit. That always makes a feller feel he'm double-crossed an' lost all friends. I mind the time well. But a couple year later, when it comes his time to strut an' drum a log, he'm addled with her ways an' can't get enough o' foolishness. It's the like o' that draws kind to kind an' makes the world go round."

They took the long way to town and Bucky showed Cam the secret banding place of the geese. Cam lingered a long time at the marsh edge.

"Another year," he said as they turned away, "I'll like to plant me a patch of corn down here. Just to see what the geese'll do. Happen I can file a claim on this stretch o' timber I'd purely like to make it a stop-over place for the geese, where they'd be safe from men an' dogs an' have a mite o' feedin'. Only God's way I could do that would be to own the land."

"Let's do it, Pa," Bucky cried. "Once we owned the land an' got 'em to come we could get help to feed an' protect 'em. Even the government would help with such as that. They've got protected places for 'em down south. We read all about 'em in school. There's a good livin' in it, too, Pa, for the fellows that start the sanctuaries."

Cam shook his head.

"'Twould take a sight o' work, Bucky, an' a sight o' money. An' we'd need the town to back us, too. Swiftwater'd never back ary plan o' the Calloways. And all the town wants is to shoot the wild birds. Look at old Hayes of the Lakeview Hotel. Promises goose huntin' in all his hotel ads. No, what we do here we got to do alone, son, like it's always been."

Bucky's gaze sought the ground and he kicked dejectedly at a leather-colored fungus. This was a plan that had been growing in his mind for a year; but he did not try to argue further.

On the way to town they shot six more partridge. Bucky brought down four of them. Two had been extra long shots and he glowed with a pardonable pride. Partridge rose like bullets from cover. A hunter got but one disappearing glimpse of them down a forest aisle and his whole being had to leap like a flame released as he sped his shot after them.

"That were close shootin'," Cam said, dropping the last bird into his sack. "Slicker'n owl grease. Now let's us hustle full-trigger to town, son, an' maybe there'll be time left to set a spell at Alf Simes' place. Aye cod, it's a long-come-short since I last heard talk turned into real conversation. Not since I last sat on Alf's porch in the summer, I'll declare."

"I like how he talks, don't you, Pa?" Bucky said.

"Wonder how come he knows such a mort o' things. He must a' passed through many a schoolhouse to know all an' shout all down, way he does."

"It ain't school learnin' that makes a feller like Alf Simes, son," Cam said. "Nor no reasy earthy. It's the man hisself. Rare as blue roses is Alf's kind, an' I mistrust he'd be the same had he never darkened a schoolhouse door."

"I hone to see Alf's tame painter cat again," Bucky said. "He'll be nigh about growed by now."

They hurried now along the trail, eager to sit awhile on Alf Simes' porch before their victualing at Stemline's store.

PROPERTY OF
FRANKFORT SCHUYLER CENTRAL
HIGH SCHOOL LIBRARY
FRANKFORT, NEW YORK 13340

7

*E*VEN IN HIS YOUNG DAYS ALF SIMES HAD SEEMED TO know a bit more than anyone else. It stood to reason, therefore, that as the gray hair and crabbedness of age crept over him he should know it all.

Having reached that time of life when active physical work is given over to others, old Alf was able to put in all his time strengthening the patriarchal position he had established in his prime. His favorite chair was on his front porch in the sun. There he would roost most of the day like some old bird, his brown, high-veined hands clutching the chair arms and his hard, bright eyes watching the wooded hills and valleys. Those eyes, alert as a fowl's, together with his harsh, sharp features and his active mind, lent him the ferine aspect that had quelled the easygoing backwoods folk. What old Alf said from his hickory chair carried a long way.

Alf's cabin was up on Hackmatack, the highest of a line of wooded hills that overlooked the lake. It was out of sight of village or neighbor and thus Alf's view was unspoiled; the few men who stopped by at intervals were the kind who smoked their pipes and

said almost nothing, letting Alf do the talking. Even
his son Hance was overawed in this respect. In spite
of his twenty-eight years, his great strength, his wife,
and his five-year-old son, Hance Simes still looked up
to old Alf as he had at fourteen. Folk down in Swiftwater said that Hance got colic pains if his pa ate a
sour apple.

In wintertime, when rheumatic twinges plagued his
lean old frame till he was grumpy as a moulting
canary, Alf would violently disavow the proven laws of
physics, even that the earth is round. The preceding
spring, when old Alf was feeling poorly, he'd had an
argument with Hen Pine, his hired man, about the moon.
The hired man had mentioned the fact that the moon
was over two hundred thousand miles away. Old Alf
had snorted and allowed that our silvery satellite hung
only a short hundred miles out in space.

For over a week they went on, fussing over the matter,
mealtimes and in between, and neither one giving
over a mile. The hired man even brought out an old almanac to prove his point, but everyone knew Alf
too well to butt in. All they could do was let things
drift.

The hired man finally saw that his job hung in the
balance. Matters were settled by splitting the difference down the middle, but veering well to Alf's side,
which allowed the moon about ten thousand miles lee-
way from the earth, one of the few compromises Alf
ever made.

Another of old Alf's confutations was on the matter
of the centuries. The whole world needed to be set
right on the subject of time. Here we are calling this
the twentieth century when any fool could see we were
still in the first half of the nineteenth.

Back in the summer that argument had come up and
it had been Cam Calloway and Wiley Meeks who

stood out against Alf longer than any of the others. But it was no use trying for a toe hold when Alf got high-fire. Time after time Wiley would start out with the first century and carry the argument forward one step at a time, but always around the seventh or eighth century Alf would confound him. Night after night they'd thrashed the thing out.

"Now take me," Cam would say. "While I call myself forty-three year old, I'm already in my forty-fourth year, which I been ever since my last birthday."

"You are, huh? You sit an' tell me you was a year old the day you was born?" old Alf would cry.

"Not that, not that—" Cam would shake his head.

"You fellers can't even figger up to forty," Alf would bristle. "An' it's the same with them centuries. Hist'ry was wrote down by a pack o' tomfools, somewheres back in the beginning, the which is a cussid shame."

It went on that way all through the hot weather, but they couldn't budge old Alf. The last two weeks Cam had drawn out of it, admitting himself punch-drunk from punishment and beaten to a feather-edged frazzle. Meeks held out to the bitter end, but it got so he did little but spit between the railings and off the porch, all in one spit. Finally one night toward September Meeks broke down completely.

"I give over," he said. "But I still feel somethin' dang well happened to one o' them doggone centuries!"

That had been a big day for Tamarack Hill. Bucky had been there, sitting quiet by Cam's knee on the second step of Alf's porch. He had long since lost track of the argument but he continued nevertheless to be fascinated by Simes' oratory. Neither Cam nor Bucky had seen old Alf since.

Today luck was with them. Old Alf had drawn him a good house; his sagging old porch was crowded with listeners till the underpinning swayed. The old man was in fine fettle, but he broke off smack in the middle of a sentence at sight of Cam. Though the two didn't always jibe, Cam was one of old Alf's greatest admirers.

"How do, Cam?" he called out. "Proud to see you here. It's long since you set on my porch. Too long. How's your health?"

"Howdy," Cam said. "Why, I'm prime an' superfine this fall weather. Been travelin' a mite—down east to the French lakes—or I'd a' stopped by long gone."

Alf hailed Cam right up to a special seat beside the big drum. Bucky slipped unnoticed around to the kitchen to look at the panther old Alf had caught up on Sugarloaf Mountain. Alf kept the cat in a wooden cage that had a door opening into the kitchen. Sometimes he'd shove food into it, and sometimes he let the cat come out. He kept it more to arouse criticism, some thought, than because he had a liking for the animal.

The big cat bared dirklike fangs at Bucky and hunkered down in a corner, its yellow-notch eyes pinned to the boy's face with basilisk fixity. Presently it began racing back and forth, turning and twisting till one marveled how it kept itself hair-side out. Bucky soon tired of watching it and sought the porch.

Alf had set out today to prove that the earth was neither round nor movable. He was summing up his arguments now, for Cam's benefit.

"Here, let's take us a workin' hy-potheosis," he cried. "You got to have one to prove anything, as poor Wiley Meeks proved to us back in the summer. Now take these altitude records they been makin'. Them balloonists went up from a given p'int, didn't they? Reckon you'll all take that as a talkin' p'int, won't you?" Alf swept all present with his Argus stare.

The listeners nodded.

"Well, them fellers stayed up ten to twenty-four hours an' made their records an' they come down again. An' where did they come down? In Siberia, China, or the South Seas? No, sir. They come down within a mile of where they went up. An' what had this t'restral ball been doin' all them hours, whirlin' round an' round like a chicken with its head off, like these science sharps like to believe? No. She'd been settin' here flat an' solid like she's always set an' always will, an' it wouldn't a' mattered if they'd stayed up a week. They'd still a' come down in the same place. What's that prove? W'y, the Bible itself speaks of the four corners of the earth, don't it? Has a whirlin' ball got corners?"

Ira Eddy, who'd read many a book and could juggle uncommon words on occasion, held out for a time.

"It all sounds right laudable, way you tell it, Alf, but 'twouldn't never prove feasible, come to a test," he said sagely.

Laudable, feasible. They had it back and forth hammer and tong for a time, confounding the company on the plain matter of words. But old Alf had the cute of it. It wasn't only feasible, he said; it was provable, and plausible.

"The Swiftwater teacher'd never hold with you," Ira Eddy said.

"That feller!" Alf snorted. "He's set on this porch before now, don't never think he ain't. W'y, he's hardly sure what's three times seven from one week to another. Went home from here with his tail hangin' like a wet wolf's, last time he stopped by."

Old Alf talked on till there wasn't a murmur of opposition left. After that he just ran on, touching on history, showing up how the president had made many a fool move the past year that a man like Alf could have turned into a coup, giving mankind and most of its institutions a good raking over in a way that got laughs out of men whose mouths hadn't turned up in the last decade. It was edging on dark when the company broke up.

"Come back one day soon, Cam," Alf called.

"I'll do that," Cam promised.

"You think old Alf's right an' the teacher an' the geography books is wrong?" Bucky asked after a time.

"I wouldn't go for to say he was, this time, but bedogged if I rightly care," Cam chuckled. "The thing is, we heard more an' better talk than we known since last we set on his porch."

Down at Stemline's store a big surprise awaited them. Cam's traps had arrived that day, two dozen Whitehouse Number Fives and Eights. In the excitement their victualing was sketchy, and they even cut short their stay in town. Within half an hour they were headed home, each laden with a heavy, clanking sack. And that night Cam worked late before the open fire, cleaning his old traps and oiling the new.

8

CAM HAD ONLY ONE GUIDING TRIP THAT FALL. MR. Corey Tate, wealthy lumberman from Bangor, showed up as usual on the first day of deer season and he and Cam spent four days in the woods, stalking deer and hunting wild birds. It netted Cam sixty dollars. At the end of that time an unseasonable cold spell set in, the wild birds decamped for the South, and even the deer removed to winter-yard in their secret places in the deep woods.

One early morning in mid-November Cam came into the kitchen with a pail of spring water clinking with ice. Bucky was just sousing his face and hands at the kitchen sink.

"Well, we got our work cut out for us today, son," Cam said.

Bucky's heart sank. More wood, he guessed. They had been cutting up winter wood for the past three days.

"Figger to set out our new trap line clear up the Jack-pine 'fore night."

Bucky's face emerged from the towel, eyes glowing.

"It'll snow by afternoon," Cam announced. "Just the day for some real clever trap an' snare work. Snow'll come on an' cover all our sets by night. An' all them wild critters in there figgerin' the world's their own. We'll make an all-fired big catch, first night. So hurry on with your breakfast, son, 'less you want I should go alone—"

"Now Pa, you wouldn't!" Bucky cried. He sped to his place at the table. As he ate cakes and bacon he looked out the window. The pine tops were bending before a cold north wind. The gray sky was darkening to slate color.

"I already cut up the bait," Cam said. "We'll take along the rifle. Might be we can gun us that sneakin' varmint that was trailin' us last time."

"You can gun us some more meat while you're at it," Ma Calloway said. "We're fresh out again."

She was busy wrapping corn bread and bacon in paper to put in Cam's knapsack. Cam went outside again to chain up old Sounder, for he wanted no noise or fear of dogs to rouse the wild dwellers in the new secret valley.

The traps were already in their canvas sacks. Just before they started Cam stuffed several hundred feet of heavy leather thongs in his sack.

"It's a long way, so don't expect us back till full dark," he said, swinging the knapsack over one shoulder and the sack of traps over the other. They set out, Bucky weaving slightly under his load of more than sixty pounds of trap iron.

"Don't let Sounder loose till close on to dark," Cam called over his shoulder.

They wasted no time in talk today, nor did they tarry once along the trail, though from time to time Bucky had to stop and lower his sack and get his breath. Both were dressed in thick brown linsey-woolsey and wore heavy felt shoes, the soles of which never slipped and were almost noiseless on the forest floor.

In a little more than an hour they reached the entrance to the valley and once in that dark, forbidding tangle a hush seemed laid upon them. Bucky felt, as on that first day, an overshadowing sense of oppression.

Cam set to work at once planting artful sets along the stream bed and up the larger ravines. At least half the traps he laid were blind sets, unbaited and buried shallowly in earth or leaves. His mink and otter sets were placed in the stream itself, traps covered with mud, the trap pans level with the surface of the water. Later these would be camouflaged with ice and snow till they looked like half-submerged stones. He used wire snares for ermine.

"Easiest way to catch them little dobbers is to lay out chunks of iron on the snow, smeared with grease. No weasel can keep from lickin' bacon grease. His tongue freezes to the iron as he licks an' he dies a slow, tormented death. Many a one I've seen dyin' in torture thataway. It's a sorry, low-down trick for a man to play. I never come onto a bait like that but I take it up or chunk it in a stream. Another place I draw the line is strychnine," Cam added. "I just won't be a party to poisonin' in the woods."

Among the blow-downs and drift jams in the stream bed Cam devised crafty snares, log falls and spring traps of bent saplings held by thongs, which often proved more efficient than traps of steel. Bucky watched each process in the rapt silence of a neophyte learning from a master. In every instance Cam went where an animal would likely go. He seemed to think and plan like a wild thing itself. At one sheltered place between three trees he constructed a crude lean-to shelter of bark for the future storing of traps.

As they penetrated farther up the valley both father and son felt again that they were not alone. At times Cam would pause in his work and stand motionless, listening. Bucky wished his father would talk, but Cam remained silent.

As they rested from their work at midday, both suddenly became aware of someone near them, watching from behind. Leaning against a tree, as if he had sprung out of limbo, was a short, dark-clad man, empty-handed, with a swart face and bright eyes, which by their odd expression seemed empty of everything but distant thought.

"Hello, Nigosh." Cam's tone was both startled and relieved.

"Layin' traps, hey? Fur sign pooty good in here. Mm. Yeah," said Indian Peter Nigosh in a voice as quiet as the dusk beneath the trees. "But mebbe ye better let 'em be. . . . Nex' season. You wait."

The Indian was already passing on.

Cam stood up. "Why?" he called after Nigosh.

"How your old line round the lake?" Nigosh replied. "Bucky want line of his own now? . . . Mm. Yeah. Thought so. Bad dog in here now. You see."

He disappeared through the trees along the stream bank. It was Nigosh's way to come and go suddenly. They heard his voice once more, out of the shadows.

"Mebbe all right in here nex' season. You wait."

Then he was gone, a shadow among shades, troubling the quiet of the forest so little as hardly to have been there.

There was a long silence before Bucky spoke.

"What'd Nigosh mean, bad dog, Pa?"

"It's the Injun term for a trap robber, in a way o' speakin'," said Cam. A troubled shadow crossed his face.

"Think it was Nigosh watchin' us that first day?" Bucky asked.

Cam thought a moment. "No," he said finally. "But it's mortal queer."

"Maybe Nigosh wants this range for himself," Bucky said.

"No. That ain't his way. Always been a good friend to us, Nigosh, an' the Micmacs never hunted in here. . . . Somethin' he knows. But we ain't to be drove from this valley, whether or no."

Bucky was taken aback by the sudden heat of the statement, but Cam spoke no more on the matter. They went on. At midday, as they ate a sketchy lunch, the first dry snow began slanting through the pines on the wings of the northwest wind. Cam seemed elated.

"Couldn't o' picked a better day," he said. "Time we're turnin' home even our tracks'll be covered."

But Bucky couldn't rejoice, not under the shadow of these trees.

It was two hours later, as they were coming out of the valley, the snow already an inch deep, that misfortune fell. They were threading the rocks along the stream bed when Cam's foot went out from under him on the icy snow. He fell sprawling, and a boulder that had stood poised on another rock for untold years was dislodged by his weight, toppling to crush his leg.

Bucky, who was ahead, heard his father's stifled gasp of pain. He turned to see Cam crumpled on the ground, his two hands grasped in agony about his lower leg. For a space the boy stood rooted in his tracks. Then Cam's voice released him.

"Bad luck! The bone's broke!" His voice was a croak.

Bucky knelt in fright to raise his father, but Cam's hand held him back. A strange, waxen pallor had spread

round his eyes and forehead as he fought against faint-
ing. The stabbing anguish of the pain that shot through
his limb had numbed the very roots of will. He propped
himself with a hand on the ground, sat deathly still for a
space, his breath rasping like a runner's. Then he spoke.

"It's bad, son. Go find two strong strips o' pine bark.
An' bring a length o' thong."

Sobbing under his breath, Bucky darted away among
the trees, stumbling, searching with half-seeing eyes for
he hardly knew what. The forest, to which he and Cam
had always been attuned, had suddenly turned against
them, implacable, remorseless; it had struck Cam down,
swift as a bolt of light.

When Bucky got back Cam sat in a daze of pain, his
back to a tree. Sweat stood in beads on his forehead. He
looked up.

"Tie that thong round my foot, son. E-easy does it . . .
there. Now tie the other end round that saplin' there.
Tie it tight."

In a minute Bucky had the knots secure.

"Got to pull against the thong now to set the bones in
place," Cam said.

"Oh, Pa, shouldn't I go for help? Doc Waters—"

"There ain't time," Cam said. "Got to do it ourselves
before the swellin' starts, or I'll be crippled for life."

Cam began to pull back slowly. It took a gigantic
effort of will, and in the agony of it his breath came
panting from his lips. He groaned and Bucky, kneeling
close, prayed, his face turned up to the pine boughs.
Finally, with a nauseating click, the bones snapped into
place. Then for a merciful moment Cam's head sank on
his chest; consciousness waned.

When he came to his thin face was lined with pain, his
mouth grim and wry: "The valley's got in the first lick,"
he said.

A dark shaft entered Bucky's chest at the words, but he closed a gate against it, threw it off.

"Does it pain bad, Pa?"

"Like a bear'd sunk his teeth into the bone an' hung on." Cam propped his back against the tree again. "We set it, good as we can. 'Twon't swell so much now. Now lay them bark strips round the leg, son, hollow side in, an' bind a thong round 'em."

Bucky jumped up from where he knelt.

"Break away the edges," Cam said. "They got to fit close together. Got to act as a cast till the doc can get to me. Easy now. Pull the thong tighter as I tell you, a leetle at a time."

Bucky obeyed with trembling hands. Cam winced and groaned aloud, but at last the crude cast was tight in place.

"Next thing's to get home," Cam said. "You better go back now and fetch a sled. Our wood sled'll do, I reckon. But maybe you'd best stop an' bring Jeth Mellott back with you. It'll be hard pullin' me over the humps an' hollows."

"I'll get him."

"Take the hand ax first an' cut a few pine boughs an' pile 'em over me. It'll keep off the snow. We're in for real weather."

"Want I should start you a fire?" Bucky said when this was done.

"No need. Get goin', son, an' hurry."

Homeward through the dim aisles between the trees Bucky sped long-legged, at a sort of Indian lope. The snow was thicker now, setting in for an all-night storm. But it wasn't the snow that dimmed his vision. Tears of misery and grief ran down his cheeks and his tortured mind roved afar, coping with a score of dire possibilities. Cam lying back there suffering, perhaps crippled, and the hopes of the family shattered again. He sped faster, trying to shed the picture.

The dark trees passed him by in somber procession. His legs pumped up and down endlessly, but his progress seemed snail-slow. But he did not slacken his pace even after his heart fell to pounding.

His whole being cried out, framing a plea to the wilderness. It was like a prayer, but all that came forth was a single sobbing word.

"Please—" he breathed to the surrounding trees and the growing night.

Dusk was coming on when he reached the home clearing. The sled on which they hauled their winter wood was by the shed. He took up the rope, and jerked the frozen runners loose. He did not stop to tell Ma, but took the trail that led to the Mellott cabin.

It was full dark and he was nearly spent when he came to the house on the Shoulder. There was yellow lamplight within, and a plume of smoke curled from the chimney. Bucky thumped at the door. He must have been leaning against the jamb in his exhaustion, for he almost fell inside when Mrs. Mellott opened.

"Why it's Bucky Calloway! Whatever's wrong?" she cried. "Jeth, come up here."

Big Jeth Mellott climbed up through a trap door from the cellar. Bridie, in a blue apron, hurried in from the kitchen.

"Well, well, Bucky, come in, come in! Don't stand there in the cold," Jeth called out in his foghorn voice.

Bucky came only a step or two inside. "It's Pa," he gasped. "He's lyin' 'way up in the Jackpine with a broke leg—"

The Mellotts clustered about him shutting off his words, all but old Mrs. Bates, Bridie's grandma, who sat on by the fire stonily silent. New panic surged up in

Bucky at the incredulity on all their faces in this safe, warm, lighted room.

"How'd he come by it?" Jeth had to know.

"A big boulder—it tipped over an' caught him as we come down the creek. Please help me get him out, Jeth! I got our sled outside."

Bridie's father roused to action. "I'll go hitch up Agatha."

"The trees are too thick in there," Bucky said. "We couldn't never get to him with a rig. We'd best take the hand sled."

"Guess you're right. But somebody's got to go fetch Doc Waters."

"I'll drive in and get him while you're bringing Cam out," Bridie said. She hurried to get her coat. Jeth was already pulling on his Mackinaw.

"All this food," Mrs. Mellott said. "We were just about to sit. Can't somebody eat a bite?"

"I can and will," said Grammer Bates, who was already seated at the table. "Good food never went to waste in my time, come high water or Indians."

"It'll wait for us," Jeth said. "We got to hurry. Cam might freeze to death, night like this. Now where's that lantern?"

Bucky leaped to the door at Bridie's side. "I'll help hitch," he said, grateful for any action. A measure of relief was already flooding over him. Help was on the way.

A vast sense of gratitude to the Mellotts came over him. Bridie—she wasn't all fool in spite of her ruffles and silliness. Still near as good as a man when she wanted. Her hands were quicker and surer than his in the dimness of the barn, buckling Agatha's harness. Take her for a grown woman, way she turned to him as Jeth came out with the lantern: "No use to fret so, Bucky. We're doing all that can be done."

Her words and the look she gave him stilled the turmoil in his chest. He thought about that again and again as he and Jeth plodded northward in the flickering circle of the lantern light.

9 ~~~~~~~~~~~~~~~~

*F*OR THREE DAYS AFTER CAM'S ACCIDENT, IT SNOWED
intermittently. The slate-black clouds of winter had
banked up in the north and west. They were moveless,
changeless, remote, and mackereled like banks of cor-
rugated metal, and the only sun the family saw was a yel-
lowish filter at midday that came in the cabin window
like a thin sifting of sulphur dust.

It had been a grim and anxious time in the Calloway
cabin, and Bucky could hardly put his mind to anything.
Most of the time Cam had lain half asleep, sometimes
flushed with fever, sometimes with an ashen pallor, for
he had come close to pneumonia. There was little talk in
the cabin; even Ma was silent, a bad sign.

It was dusk and Bucky was just bringing in the night's
wood, enough short logs to burn till morning and a pile
of niggerheads for beside the fireplace that would last
the following day if need be. His face and ears burned
from laboring in a temperature close to forty below.
Coarse gray socks were stuffed into his felt shoes against
the cold, and a cap of worn coonskin crowned his shag-
bark hair that had not been cut in weeks. His face was

drawn and pinched, the dark eyes sullen from overwork.

Ma sat darning socks over an egg, rising now and then to stir the mush pot, or turn the cooking rabbit. Cam lay in the cord bunk in the corner of the cabin, his injured leg raised high beneath the blankets. His gaunt, unshaven face still etched with the pain he had endured before Doc Waters had come to reset the broken bone. His fever was down tonight, and worry showed in the black eyes turned up to the ceiling poles. There was little food left for the family—a few frozen rabbits in the smokehouse, a side of bacon, some beans and meal.

Bucky went out for a final log, and the door creaked behind him on its crude hinges. The snow in the clearing was almost knee-deep; the dark ring of the surrounding forest was broken only at one place, where the woods road cut like a tunnel through the pines toward town.

A sudden wind rose with the darkness. Bucky could hear it far off and high, a growing roar above the forest. Abruptly it snatched at the clearing, whirling snow in eddies. Because his impulse was to hurry in again and close the door against it, Bucky stood for several minutes with his face straight into it, letting the cold and darkness and emptiness sink into him.

Indoors, he eased down his log and took off his sheepskin coat and cap. He sat down beside Viney, who was playing with the paper people she'd cut out of the mailorder catalogue. The wind made hollow bottle noises down the chimney, and the driven snow made a dry *shish-shish* against the log walls.

"Listen to that," Ma Calloway said. "The almanac was right. We're due for a real cold spell. 'A stormy new moon. Keep a good fire,' Poor Richard says for the twentieth. 'Colder. Expect snow,' it says for the twenty-first."

Bucky's voice had a manly note. "It's getting colder all right, but it won't snow. It's too darned cold to snow. A fellow'd soon be stiff if he didn't keep working."

"Is the ax in?" Cam asked.

"Yes." Bucky fetched it and put a keen, shining edge on it with the whetstone. Then he ran a greased rag through each of the rifle barrels. He could feel his father's approving gaze on his back as he sighted through each barrel into the firelight. "Bright's a bugle." He echoed Cam's invariable comment.

Then he sat down again, waiting, his hands clasped tightly between his knees.

"Bucky," Cam said presently. The boy went over and stood dutifully by the bunk. "Do you think you can cover the trap line tomorrow, son?"

"Yes, I guess I can."

He was prickling with trepidation. The wind shook the cabin door as he spoke and he thought again of all that lay up in that far pine valley—things to be felt if not seen or heard.

"It's a long way, I know, an' it's mortal cold—" Cam's voice was drained and tired and for a moment Bucky glimpsed the naked misery and worry in his mind—"but money's scarce, son. We got to do what can be done."

"I don't mind the cold or the snow." Bucky lowered his eyes until that look should leave his father's face.

"I'll be laid up three-four weeks, maybe more. It's four days since we laid out the line. Varmints may have got most of our catch by now. You've got to go, Bucky. If you start at daylight you can make the rounds an' back by night."

"Shucks, yes." Bucky forced a smile.

When he dared lift his eyes, he saw his father's face had hardened again, coping with the problem.

"You needn't try to bring in all the catch," Cam said. "You can hang some of it on high boughs, then reset the traps. Main thing's to find what kind o' range we got in there. Later on you may have to spend a night in the valley now an' again. Think you can manage it?"

63

"Sure. I could take old Sounder for company," Bucky said largely.

Cam managed a smile. "Might have to sleep in there once every week till I'm up again. So you'd best look to that lean-to we made to store traps in. It's plenty big enough to sleep a man."

Pride filled Bucky, driving back the dread.

"You'd best eat now, son, an' turn in early," Cam said, "so's you can start at dawn."

"All right."

"You're a brave boy, Bucky," Ma said. "You're the only provider for this family now." Bucky flushed hot all over and looked away. "What a blessing it is you're big enough to cover the line while your pa's down like this. Last year you could never have done it."

"He's near about good as any man," Cam said.

Bucky felt the hair stir on his nape, the way his father said that. He grew more stolid than usual, holding against the rushing tide of feeling. He wished he were all they said of him, but he knew he wasn't. Inside he was filled with fear whenever he thought of the Little Jackpine. For three days the vision of the valley had loomed before his mind's eye, filling him with dread.

Ma was laying out the evening meal on the hewn-log table.

"Hungry tonight, Cam?"

Cam Calloway shook his head with sudden fret. "No. I can't stomach any more mush, or rabbit either. Aye gonnies, if only we had some white flour for bread."

A shadow passed over the faces of the family.

Methodically Bucky ate the man's share of food his mother set before him. Soon after, he climbed the sapling ladder to the small quarter loft, glad of the chance to grapple with his thoughts in the dark. He got in his bunk and lay still, pretending to sleep. Long after the lamp went out and the family was in bed he lay thinking, while the log fire died down till its light became a mere dancing shadow fluttering across walls and ceiling like a frightened bird trying to escape from the cabin.

Storm gripped the house in an icy clutch. The night was full of voices. The wind cried round the corners of the cabin, and the snow crept against the walls. Once, afar in the forest, a wolf howled. Bucky's skin prickled, and his hands made fists beneath the blankets.

Now and again he could hear his father sigh and stir, and he knew that Cam too was thinking about how they were going to get through the winter. And why, of all times, did he have to break his leg just after he'd run the trap line up the Little Jackpine? Bucky wouldn't have minded covering their old line along the lake shore, but that haunted valley. . . . He knew he must go, however, and he dare not show his fear or his mother would stop him. It was all up to him.

Dawn had not yet come when Bucky descended the ladder. His father was wide awake; his mother just rising. Bucky built up the fire and made coffee. He ate a hurried breakfast, then took down his old wool sweater to wear beneath his sheepskin coat.

"Make sure you don't forget anything," Cam said. "Have you got plenty cartridges, matches?"

"Yes, Pa."

"Belt ax? The clamps for the traps? Fish bait?"

"Yes."

"Best take my rifle," Cam said.

With pride Bucky took down his father's finely balanced rifle, with its curly maple stock. It was a far better weapon than the old Sharps Bucky carried; very seldom had he been allowed to use it.

"Best not take the sled," Cam said. "It's heavy and I want you should be back by dark."

There was something else that Cam seemed on the point of saying, Bucky knew as he lifted the latch. He waited a moment in the doorway, but Cam seemed to think better of it; no words came.

"You be right careful, won't you, son?" was all his father said as the door closed.

PROPERTY OF
FRANKFORT SCHUYLER CENTRAL
HIGH SCHOOL LIBRARY
FRANKFORT, NEW YORK 13340

10

THE COLD BIT DEEP. IT WAS HARDLY LIGHT YET IN THE clearing. The storm had died down in the night, and there was no actual wind now, but there was a vast rush of air out of the north that cut Bucky's cheeks like a razor. It carried bright, stinging particles on its wings; not snow, but frost. It was colder than Bucky had ever known it.

After twenty minutes of tramping he thought he would have to turn back. His face and hands were numbing, and it was an agony to snatch a breath. His eyes watered and his nose started running a mucous stream. He snatched up some of the hard, dry snow and rubbed it fiercely against his stiffened face till a faint glow of feeling came. Then he ran for a long way, beating one arm, then the other, against his body, shifting his rifle. His face was again like so much wood, and it terrified him, but he would not give up, would not turn back.

It was more than two miles to the mouth of the Little Jackpine. He covered the distance in a partial daze. The cold had all but robbed him of volition and movement. He did not know what he could do with his numbed hands if he found a catch in the traps; he could not even use the rifle if occasion arose. He would have cried had he been a year younger, but at fifteen you do not cry. He turned doggedly up the valley.

The valley had all its former threat despite the silver coating of frost that rimed every twig of the forest trees, and again there seemed something waiting, listening among the blue-black shadows. Except for an occasional snapping as the cold ate into the pithy hearts of the balsams, the silence was complete.

Bucky passed the spot where Cam's leg had been broken, but he did not dare stop, for his chest felt small and dry; and the ache in his hands and bones told of the bitter cold. After a while it seemed a bit warmer, perhaps because he was climbing. And then he came to the first trap and he forgot the snow and the cold, and even fear.

A marten, caught perhaps two days before, lay in the set. Its carcass had been partially devoured, its prime pelt torn to ribbons as if in malice. Round about were broad, splayed tracks in the snow. Wind and sleet had partly covered them so that their identity was not plain, but they told Bucky enough. It was neither foxes nor wolves that had molested this trap. Neither was it a bear.

He stood up, his eyes darting here and there for a glimpse of the secret enemy, but the dark, somber shadows of the evergreens gave back nothing. Except for the stern, forbidding mutterings of the balsam boughs overhead the stillness was complete.

His thoughts flew now to Cam. Cam would know just what to do about this. He yearned for Cam's voice, Cam's advice. Then he recalled his first real hunt. He'd been scarce thirteen then, and he and Cam were hunting partridge among the spruce jungles one afternoon, when

Cam said: "We got to connive a real hunt for you right soon, son."

That hunt came three days later, at the opening of deer season. In the mist-dank cold before the dawn they had started out, moving like two phantoms along the hardwood slopes, Bucky taut as a bowstring and hair-trigger nervous for fear he might muff something. Killing your first buck—that meant coming into manhood along the Swiftwater. Young Freeman Tedder had shot him a buck at fifteen, but no boy had ever done it going on thirteen.

It was a still hunt, an Indian hunt. As they neared the ancient feeding ground of the deer, Cam had whispered:

"Time we spread out now. You take the north slope; I'll prog over south. Feller that gets a buck first'll whistle the other in."

Silently they separated, two fledged hunters, equal and reliant on one another as the parts of one machine. It was wonderful.

Soon they were far beyond sight or sound of each other. The mist swirled in smoky streamers against a landscape vague and heroic. Everything cold and vast, the slightest sound magnified in the dawn stillness.

It wasn't near light yet when ahead of him a drifting whorl of mist stopped, moved on, and stopped again. Then bounded buoyantly down slope as the old Sharps leaped to his shoulder, gleaming steel itself. His eyes had always been keen, but that shot was a miracle, for there was neither time for eye to lower to sights, nor light to aim. Yet that which bounded through the air pitched forward with a bleat and a rattle of stones and lay bone-still. It was a fat buck, a ball through its heart; tan-gray all over like the very stuff of the dawn-dusk.

It was his faith in Cam that had won for him that morning—and all his concentration on marksmanship that had gone beyond skill into intuition. He was standing by the kill when Cam came up, the dawn just breaking so that he could see the look on his father's face.

"Six tines," Cam had muttered. "An' clean through the heart." His voice had changed. "I'll liken to call that shootin', son."

It was a thunderous encomium for Bucky, for there'd been pride in Cam's tone. He'd felt queer and almost cried.

"Reckon it startled you some when I left you back yonder," Cam had said. "But you done right; you went ahead an' didn't talk. Always remember a good hunter takes whatever the woods got in store; he asks no help an' saves his talk till later."

That was the way it had to be today. Bucky moved on between the endless ranks of the trees and again, as on the first day, he had a definite feeling of being watched. At intervals he stopped to glance back and to all sides, but there was nothing to see. The heavy trunks of the dark trees near the trail seemed to move furtively behind him. The same fearsome feeling of the first day came over him again till his feet wanted to fly away and out of the valley.

The next trap had been uncovered and sprung, the bait, a frozen fish, eaten, and the trap itself dragged away into the brush and buried in the snow. It took nearly half an hour of floundering and digging to uncover trap and clog. Hard by was another set, and there Bucky saw a thing that made his skin crawl with superstitious awe. The remains of a porcupine lay in the trap. The creature had been eaten, quills, barbs, and all. Blood was all around, blood from the jaws of the eater. Only a devil with nerves of iron or no nerves at all could have done that. Beneath a spruce where the wind had not blown the snow he saw clearly the despoiler's trail, splayed, handlike tracks like those of a small bear, each print coming to a peak of fierce claw marks.

No doubt now as to what haunted this valley. Dread seeped into the very grain and being of the timber-bred boy. Unless the creature could be outwitted or killed the trap line would be useless.

For long minutes Bucky stood in the dusky shadows, fighting down his fear. Then he thought of what awaited him at home—that stricken look in his father's face—and his fear of that was greater than his fear of the valley.

He hung his sack of frozen bait on a high bough. Useless to reset any of the traps now, for the creature he was pitted against could smell cold steel, unbaited, through two feet of snow, and was led out of sheer devilishness to rob and destroy wherever it prowled. This was the "bad dog" Peter Nigosh had spoken of. Cam had been about to tell him as he left the cabin that morning, but had refrained, hoping against hope that it wasn't true, not wanting to frighten him.

Bucky plodded on again, his chest hollow with hopelessness. He did not know what he could do, but he must go on.

The snow grew deeper. His body warmed with his exertion, grew moist, then the icy fingers of the cold found him afresh. For more than an hour he struggled on. One after another he came upon traps that had been despoiled. At the ninth trap a choked cry broke from him. Scattered about in the snow were tufts of fluffy black fur with long, silver-white guard hairs. That trap had held a prime silver fox, one of the greatest prizes known to trappers.

As he crouched there in the snow, anger jarred him to the depths. He rose and took up the endless plod again, peering into every covert in the hope of seeing a dark, skulking shape. He did not even know the size of the

71

creature. He had never seen a wolverine. Few hunters ever had, such was the wile of the beast. But there was old Laban Knowles' tale of the wolverine that had gnawed his walnut rifle stock clean in two, and scored the very rifle barrel, and Granther Bates had told of a woods devil that had killed his two dogs in fair fight, and gnawed its way through a log wall to rob him of his grub cache. Oh it was a demon right enough, whatever its size.

By midafternoon Bucky was nearing the farthest limit of the trap line. Of the twenty-odd traps he had visited only two had been unmolested. Abruptly he came upon a fresh trail in the snow: the same handlike tracks and demon claws. Grimly he turned aside to follow its twisting course.

He was descending a steep, wooded slope when on a sudden impulse he doubled in his tracks and went plunging back up the grade. As he reached the crest a dark, humped shape took form beneath the drooping boughs of a spruce. It was a ragged, sooty-black and brown beast, some three and a half feet long, that lumbered like a small bear, lighter-colored along its back and darker underneath, in direct contradiction to all other forest things. It saw him and its eyes, green-shadowed, fixed those of the boy who stood beneath a tree some hundred feet away. Its black jaw dropped open and a harsh, grating snarl cut the stillness. The utter savagery of the challenge sent a shiver through Bucky's body. His rifle flew up and he fired without removing his mitten. The whole valley roared to the thunder of the shot. In the same instant the wolverine disappeared.

Bucky rushed forward, reloading as he ran. Under the spruce were several drops of blood on the snow. But the wolverine had vanished. Because of his haste and clumsiness of the mitten, Bucky had only grazed the animal; he'd lost his one big chance.

Panting, stumbling, sobbing, he plunged along the trail, bent low, ducking under the drooping limbs of the trees, sometimes crawling on hands and knees. He saw other drops of blood. That gave him heart. He had a lynx eye on the trail, even his father said that. He would follow on to the very Circle if need be; he would not miss a second time. His one hope was to settle with the creature for good and all.

Down along the stream bed the trail led, twisting through vast tangles of windfalls, writhing masses of frost-whitened roots and branches. He tripped amid the tangles; twice he fell, but he thrust the rifle high as he went down to keep snow from jamming its snout. He plunged on again; he did not know how long, or how many miles, but he was aware at last of the afternoon nearing its end. And the end of light meant victory for the enemy.

The way had grown steeper. He was coming to the narrow throat-latch of the valley's head. A place where hundreds of pine trees, snapped off by storm and snowslide from the slopes above, had collected in a mighty log jam, a tangle of timber, rock, and snow that choked the stream bed from bank to bank. Countless logs lay criss-crossed in every direction, with two- and three-foot gaps between. The great pile was acre-large and fifty feet high; a collection of numberless years, rank with the odor of rotted wood and old snow. Into this maze the trail of the woods devil led. Bucky skirted the pile. It did not come out. Somewhere in there the creature doubtless had its lair.

Trembling, he squeezed his way into the great jam between two logs. The wolverine might be fifty yards inside, but somehow it must be ferreted out. In and in Bucky wormed his way, pausing to watch, to listen, his rifle thrust carefully before him. Then down into the twisty chaos of dead trunks, led by his nose, for the rank odor of the devil's den now filled the air coming upward from the bottom of the jam; fouler than any skunk, the taint was, the choking reek of carnivore.

A prickling sensation ran up and down the boy's spine. His distended eyes stared and darted here and there in the shadows. The dank air of the place seemed to rise up and beset him, charged with evil.

To his ears came a harsh and menacing growl, but from what direction he could not tell. He could see nothing. He loosened the safety on his rifle and wriggled forward again, and again the air was filled with that eerie challenge. A gasp was wrung from him, for this time it seemed to come from behind. He whirled in panic and there was nothing, but his terror mounted. Then still greater terror came in the suspicion that there might be two of them.

He crouched, peering, shaken to the marrow. And then movement caught his eye below and he made out a soot-dark form in the nether shadows.

Bucky wriggled on his belly along a slanting log, maneuvering for a shot. He braced himself, craning far downward, then in the very instant he took aim he slipped on the snow-sheathed log. The gun roared, the shot went wild, and as he caught himself the weapon slipped out of his grasp. It clattered downward, striking against log after log before it lodged at the bottom of the jam, snout down in snow and debris, its barrel clogged, useless.

In that instant all the supercraft that has made man master of the wild fell away and Bucky was face to face with a creature that was a direct holdover from Old Time. The wolverine was clambering upward. Inexorably it advanced upon him. He yelled at it fiercely, but there seemed not a vestige of fear in the creature's being. A sob broke from Bucky, but his hand went to his light belt ax; he did not give ground.

With a panic shout he leaned and swung at the low, flat head, but missed because of hindering logs. He swung again and again and the blade struck home, but bounced off muscles and sinews tough and unyielding as gutta-percha. The creature's advance never checked. Its fighting mask was terrible; the small, implacable eyes brimmed with a blue-green flame, as if the surface of them were burning as the surface of wood alcohol burns in a lamp.

It lunged suddenly for Bucky's dangling legs and he flung himself up and over the log, slipped on its icy sheath, and grasped desperately for another log; slipped again to bring up eight feet below. He flung round with a cry of desperation to meet open jaws, feeling the demon almost upon him. But the thing was logy and slow. Its might lay in its indomitability and a slow, resistless strength.

In it came again, above him now. He stood upright, braced on two logs, to meet it.

He struck again, yelling with every blow of the belt ax, but hack and cut as he would the beast's wounds seemed to have no effect upon it. It bore in and in. Leechlike, it maneuvered along the undersides of logs to avoid the ax blows, always coming on.

Then Bucky slipped again, avoiding the traplike jaws. He fell clear to the bottom of the jam, biting snow as he screamed. He was on his feet again before the creature above released its claw hold and dropped upon him like a giant slug.

An arm flung up over his throat, he jerked back blindly, and just in time. Spread saber claws tore open his heavy coat. Then the ax fell again, blow after blow with all his strength.

The thing came up at him in spite of all. The jaws lanced in and clamped on his leg and he felt his own warm blood. Then his hand found the skinning knife at his belt and the blade sank deep in the corded neck—sank and turned till the clamp of jaws released.

Then up out of the abatis Bucky climbed till half his body emerged and there he rested, panting, spent. He whimpered once, but there wasn't a tear in his eye. Those eyes had a jumping light, and one could have seen back through them like an open window into a fearsome country one had never seen before. Instinctively they lifted skyward. Overhead, as night drew on, had come a great rift in the dull canopy of cloud and a few stars shone faintly through. He held his eyes on the brightest star, until chaos left them and their vision steadied, cleared, as if his head were higher up than ever it had been before, in a realm of pure air. His brain was almost frighteningly clear.

The trickle of warm blood down his leg roused him. He pressed his heavy pant leg round his wound till he felt the bleeding slow. Soon it would congeal. Painfully he turned down into the maze of logs again and after a time brought up the rifle. Then down again to struggle upward, dragging the woods devil itself. He laid it out on the snow and brought forth his bloody knife. He wasn't tired now; he wasn't cold; he wasn't afraid. His hands were quick and sure at the skinning; even his father had never lifted a pelt with smoother, defter hand. Darkness shut down as he worked, but he didn't need light. There wasn't any hurry. The head he cut off and left intact, attached to the pelt.

He rose at last and rolled up his grisly bundle, fur side out, and moved away through the blackness of the trees, sure of tread, for he had the still-hunter's "eyes in the feet." The reflection from the snow gave a faint light. He limped a bit as he turned homeward.

Off in the black woods a wolf howled dismally and Bucky smiled. Never again would the night dogs make his skin crawl. Never again would he be afraid of anything above ground.

PART TWO

11 ~~~~~~~~~~~~~~~~~~~

𝒥OR FOUR WEEKS AFTER THE KILLING OF THE WOLVER-
ine, the hide of the woods devil hung pegged to the
Calloways' log wall for all who stopped by to see. It
was Cam himself who insisted on this. Pride rose in him
like a yeast over Bucky's exploit, for none knew better
than he the craft and mettle of this demon beast and all
the boy had overcome in the valley—things that would
never come out in words. Pride glowed in Bucky, too,
a quiet and tempered thing that steadied and strength-
ened like strong food in the belly, for it had its roots in
things conquered and achieved.

Scraped, dried, and softened to the pliancy of buck-
skin, the devil's hide was pegged beside the fireplace.
When the word got round outlying neighbors came
daily to see the thing and to hear the tale from Bucky's
own lips. Men from as far north as Otter Run made
trips to the Calloway place just to see the skin, for
not a hunter in the Swiftwater country had ever shot
or trapped a wolverine, or ever caught more than fleeting glimpse of one.

"Think there might be two of 'em in the valley, Pa?" Bucky had asked the first night.

"Two nothin'!" Cam snorted. "Ain't room in the woods for two o' him. Them devils war on each other, too, tooth an' tong. Even mates will fight to the death at times. Feller never finds but one of 'em on any range."

Cam disclosed then how he had felt from the first that a woods devil haunted the valley and had been certain of it after Peter Nigosh's warning, but had refrained from telling Bucky. He told of how the little Aleuts of the far North strove to obtain a hunting coat of wolverine skin as a badge of craft and bravery and a symbol of arrived manhood. And of tales he had heard of a tribe in far-off Africa where boys achieved manhood only by killing a lion.

Cam was all for preserving the devil skin intact. Later they could have glass eyes put in the head. But Bucky craved a cap of wolverine fur, so Cam said no more. It was Bucky's treasure.

Finally, when folk stopped coming, Ma Calloway set to work on the hide. There was enough for a pair of mittens in the bargain. With the cap of rough, coarse brownish fur crowning his unshorn head, Bucky looked like some shaggy untamed woods creature that had crept in by the fire. Shorter and shorter were his stays by the fire now, for all the life of the family depended upon him.

Bucky was sixteen now, two weeks gone. Already he was taller than Cam, but scantling thin, what with work and worry. The first fuzz of manhood's beard was beginning to show along his lean cheek. Wild as a lynx cat, people down in Swiftwater said of him, shy as the brown willow wren which folk only hear and never see. Townfolk caught only fleeting glimpses of Bucky these days, trading a hide for victuals at Stemline's store, or streaking through the woods. Most times his fierce, thin face wore a stoic gravity, but underneath one might catch at times a glancing as of flame hidden in a dark vessel—the glow of youth repressed.

Cam still lay in his bunk deep sunk in misery. For another month at least he must chafe in idleness, waiting the time when Doc Waters would let him try out his slowly mending leg. And even then it would be a time before he could trek the woods. So much to be done, so brief the time to do it in, and this the high tide of the winter trapping season.

Bucky was bowed beneath the care of the trap line and all the chores—trying to act like he was Cam, holding hard against the undermining of exhaustion and that subtler gnaw of self-importance, that vaunting and being puffed up that the Good Book warned against. Owl-serious he was, hardly laughing even at Ma's jokes, keeping tab of his catch with stub of pencil, chunking firewood on the hearth with unguarded noise and patriarchal sigh, polishing gun barrels till they shone, whetting ax to razor edge, trying not to show the fierce rioting of his mind. He hunted early and late to keep the family in meat and often he rated Viney, who asked him endless foolish questions out of admiration.

No greater champion had Bucky now than Viney. Each new harvest of fur built Bucky up in the worshipful eyes of his sister; each night spent in the lonely blackness of the deep woods, which Viney shuddered even to think about. Always there'd been a deep bond between these two, nonetheless binding because it was wordless, or cloaked in the disparagement of sixteen for nine. But now Bucky knew and Viney knew the depth of that attachment.

A man now in all but siring, with Ma constantly at his shoulder, each the other's staunch lieutenant. Never a complaint or jaw word out of Ma these days, nor any reading of the law. Always Ma's sounding off had been reserved for the unimportant times. Now life flowed through her calm and strong and silent as the current down a big river. She was strong; she knew how to struggle, Ma did. Never one to resign herself. She even found occasion to make her special kind of jokes at times, which always brought a chuckle out of Cam. Her good nature was like another fire in the house, keeping back the chill of worry as the pitch-pine logs kept at bay the frost.

She was never idle. When all housework was done and a pot of something stood "simperin'" on the fire, she'd sit down and help with the skins Bucky brought in, stretching them on their wooden forms, scraping and softening them by the open fire, kneading them to the pliancy of suede, brushing their piled nap till they glowed with the luster of perfection. All evening her rocker went *eek-and-ok* on the uneven plank before the hearth, while she bent engrossed over her work.

"Throw another stick on, Viney. I can't quite see to foller my blade," she would say.

Too full of twist and go to be still, Viney too was set to the scraping and softening. Even Cam lying in his bunk could help with this—a godsend. Carefully he examined every pelt that Bucky spilled from his filled sack of an evening with expert appraisal and often with a word of praise, while Bucky stood by with the faint sweat of pride on his frost-darkened face. Cam would hold the pelts up, blowing expertly into the piled nap, estimating their value—each skin a rare mint of the secret woods.

"How many now, son?" he would ask and Bucky, who kept careful record, would study his list.

"Forty-two, Pa. Twenty-four of 'em prime number ones, I figger. Worth up to twenty-five dollars apiece at Stemline's."

"We're gettin' out o' the woods for fair," Cam would say. "Spite o' me lyin' here hog-tied an' halted. Ol' Hard Luck went an' hunted him another range, after layin' me low. Couldn't cope with you nohow, Bucky."

"'Bout time we drew an easy breath or two," Ma would say.

Bucky would flush and say, "I aim to have more skins a-curin' here than a body'll know what to do with, come January. There's another little valley branchin' out o' the Jackpine. We was hindsighted not to seen it sooner. Happen our catch keeps good, I could buy me more traps and work up there. We'd soon pay off all debts then. But Viney or some'un would have to do the chorin' here. I'd not have the time."

"Was I you, I'd connive to simmer down a mite an' eat an' rest more," Ma would warn, eying Bucky's thin back bent above a pelt. "You'm purely gaunted up from work an' worry."

"Work's good for the boy," Cam said. "It's the makin' of ary man."

"If 'twas that good the rich would 'a takened it over long since," Ma retorted.

The skins kept coming in. Three looped chains, suspended from a beam of the storehouse against the inroad of rodents, were weighted with them and the cabin walls were pegged from floor to rafter. The Jackpine Valley, now free of devils, was giving up a daily tithe of treasure, richer than any take Cam could remember even in his luckiest years. There was food aplenty in the cabin—meat and side pork, bacon and beans, flour for bread and flapjacks, even maple sirup, and canned goods galore.

By mid-December there were otter, mink, and marten skins stretched and curing; two cross foxes, and two grays, the pelts of six gray timber wolves, three lynx skins, and five black and gleaming fisher skins, worth a whole season's work to any trapper. Always these had been Ma Calloway's special love. For years she had dreamed and talked of having a cape of fisher skins someday, with maybe a muff to match. But never an extra look did she give them. Never a hait did she care, it appeared, how many skins they pegged up to cure.

Cam watched from his bunk, his eyes twinkling at times. Then one morning, when Ma had gone to the root cellar, he called Bucky to his bunk. An hour later Bucky was on his way to the Mellott cabin, carrying with him the cream of the Calloway fur harvest: the five glossy fisher skins, and with them a pretty gray-fox pelt as a gift to Mrs. Mellott, who had no little fame in the region as a seamstress and a deft worker with fur. It was a reckless thing to do with the family's many outstanding debts, but there is nothing like a long, close-up tussle with poverty to make men prodigal of their first winnings. Cam and Bucky were agreed. Christmas was not far round the corner now, and Ma was to have her cape at last, whether or no.

12 ~~~~~~~~~~~~~~

*T*HAT WINTER, COLD WAS MORE THAN A WORD. MID-
December was a whole series of heavy snows, with days
of still cold in between. When the sun shone at all it
was not centered, but surrounded by a great wan halo
half as wide as the zenith, out of which lurid sundogs
flared, warning of further storms to come.

But the Calloways' winter wood had been cut in summer, and stacked against shed and cabin wall for the hot
sun to season, so now there was fuel in abundance. All
day the stovelids were red, and all night a banked log
in the fireplace kept the frost at bay. But only by a
matter of shrinking feet. A white rime of frost thickened round latch and cabin door each night, and the
panes of the double windows gradually grew opaque
under a quarter inch of ice and frost, which melted
only a mite at noontime and froze the thicker for it
after dark. Old Laban Knowles, who had been deepen-
ing his root cellar, said that the frost stabbed better
than four feet into the earth, nigh as deep as any grave.

On still days an unearthly calm seemed to have set-

tled over the land and the snap of a twig carried almost
a mile. By night the frost probed into the hearts of the
pine till they cracked and moaned at times, filling the
silence with the strange, protesting voices of inanimate
things. Often the cabin timbers snapped with a sound
like small pistol shots.

With the cold came the wolves, more than anybody on
the Swiftwater could mind for many a year. Like the
spirits of the snow, they came in closer as the cold increased. They came round outlying homesteads after
dark, thick as crows in summertime, the smaller brown
wolves of the plains country with their yapping ulula-
tions and the big gray timber wolves from farther north
that howled in banshee chorus nightly, near and far.
'Twas not moon baying, as some liked to believe, for
they howled closer on the blackest nights. 'Twas the
hunger call, Cam said, aimed to addle the wits and
nerves of all small game of the thickets with fear.

"It's eight year or more since I heard that devils' song
so close," he said.

Ma would stand only a few minutes of their carrying
on around the place, then she'd go out the door and
whack a fire stick against the cabin wall till they'd stop.

Bucky had no fear of them now. Since his ordeal in
the valley there was not even a smidgin of dread left
in him. Long since, Cam had taught him that an able-
bodied man had nothing to fear from wolves, despite
the lurid tales that were written about them. They'd
follow a man like any cur, but keep their distance. They
knew well the difference between a man with a gun
and a man unarmed.

Old Scissorbill the crow never left his cage these
days. He sat there hunched, ill-natured and accusing,
in his rusty black, with a mortal fear in his hard old eye
whenever cabin door was opened. He'd set on being a

convalescent till spring, had Scissorbill, and now Ma must feed him and clean up after him like another patient in the house. Old Sounder too clung close to the fire, refusing to go outside till rated and stirred with a boot toe.

And Keg was another problem for a time. He bawled and scratched at door and window, miserable and put-upon, pleading to be cabin-bound like the rest of the family. But Ma Calloway was adamant. She drove him back to his place in the deep root cellar, now empty of stores, where he whined and mumbled for some days. All his instincts leaned toward sleep as the snows came heavier, but all of it was vague as vague, a mere whisper in the blood, for he'd never been taught the snug habit of hibernation. But gradually Nature took over for him. He now gave over eating entirely.

For a time the family worried about him, but 'twas neither death nor sickness that had come upon him. Gradually, as the snows and cold increased, he fell into torpid sleep from which he roused only for a few minutes every two or three days. Several times each day Bucky or Viney looked in on him fearing he would freeze, but his heavy fur and the heat from his own fat body took care of that, tempering the air of the small dugout. Heavy snow soon lay over the roof and walls of the root cellar and banked against the plank door and Keg slept on, as snug as in any cave the deep woods might have offered.

Cam chuckled when he heard.

"He's free o' worry for the winter now, an' so are we. He'll sleep an' dream an' do a sight o' growin' there till April, an' come out a larrupin' big bruiser well-nigh growed an' wonderin' what's come over him. He'll take to the wild, I mistrust, come berry time."

After the third heavy snow Viney had to stay home

from school, for the drifts had become waist-high on a man, so now there was a third pair of hands for curing pelts.

Bucky had reason to believe there was another black fox or two on the new range. He had seen fresh fox sign after each new snow. He had also seen the broad round tracks of old Fire Eyes, the Swiftwater panther, known to every settler in the region for his bloody raids on outlying farms. Evenings he and Cam held councils of war in the cabin. Cam could envision every foot of the valley and the winding stream at its bottom. Even lying there abed he knew all the likeliest spots to snare a fox.

"Is the stream froze over?" he asked.

"Better than half is under an inch of ice. But up above there's plenty open water."

"Try can you find an open stretch where the foxes come to drink," Cam said. "Likely you'll find a stone there, out in the water a foot or two from shore. A fox is everly p'tic'lar about his drinkin'. He favors restin' his forefeet on a stone in the water while he laps his fill. It's there you can outsmart Mr. Fox with a waterset. A black fox is smart as a treeful of owls at smellin' out traps. Twice as sharp as ary gray an' well nigh as slick as a woods devil at catchin' the man scent. But a water set carries no scent. Happen you can plant your set on a rock that's just under water you'll get your fox. Come next storm the trap pan'll look like a nubbin o' rock covered over with ice an' snow. Some fox is bound to put his foot on it for a last drink."

The next day Bucky found just such a drinking place as Cam had described. A flat rock at the stream bank was half submerged in water. It was as though Cam had visited the place in spirit and seen all beforehand.

Bucky laid his trap and came away hoping for another snow to camouflage his work.

For catching a prowling panther, Cam said, the surest way was a spring-gun set; a loaded rifle should be set in dense brush, with a cord leading from the trigger to a fresh-killed grouse or rabbit, placed in direct line of the sights.

"A painter cat is purely addle-pated. He'm the cat that curiosity killed, as the feller said, an' he'm bound to examine ary bait that's laid out. The rest is up to the gun."

Bucky listened to all in rapt attention.

Talk of traps and woods lore was only a part of the wonder of the winter evenings of late. Ma had cannily set aside three nights a week for family reading, during this period when Cam must keep to his bed. These were red-letter nights for all, a time of celebration.

Oil was a scarce thing and often the family's only evening light was the glancing glow of the open fire. Even their evening meal was eaten in this partial shadow, but their hands knew well the road to their mouths. But on these special nights, Ma would bring down the Radiant Beam from its place on the shelf, and put it on the center table. Its golden glow would light up the whole big room, even to the smoke-darkened ceiling poles. Then she would bring out the great brass-bound family Bible from its shelf and there would be reading aloud for an hour or more.

Ma would invariably start it, with serious mien, forging haltingly through a chapter or so, wrestling with many a word and phrase. Finally Cam would take over. He had the heart and the voice for it. Great was the lift in their spirits that came from an hour with Scripture.

With the great book propped on his chest, Cam would

roll out story after story in a sonorous voice that made the cabin ring. Cam did not "wale a portion," but took Old Testament as it came.

"King David, he played the tomfool. Women," he said one night. " 'Twas the same with old King Solomon, only more so. Old Solomon was more than a grain wise, by all account, an' the big rabbit in the turnip patch back there in Israel, but a cold-out strollop for all that. More than a thousand hussies he had hid away in his great palace an' a mighty stand o' young'uns, they say. Reckon even Talt Bingham up on Hat Creek could a' took pointers from him."

"An' likely did," Ma said. "Talt's purely replenishin' the country in the good old Bible way."

"An' there was Old Man Adam," Cam went on. "He started the line of 'em. The whole book of beget an' begat stemmed from him."

"One o' them fellers was bad as t'other by far," said Ma seriously. "But don't forget Old Man Noah," she added acidly. "Biggest fool o' the lot. He got drunk." Her eyes glinted momentarily at her man.

"Yes, the pore benighted dobber; he had to go an' press out the first grapes." Cam avoided her glance. "But later he walked with God, 'tis said."

Few characters of the Book escaped some sharp disparagement from Cam. Paul and Moses were among these few. Of Moses he never ceased his praise.

"Fancy all these writin' fellers rackin' head an' his-t'ry book for some tale startlin' enough to tell, an' there's old Moses, greatest hero of all time, with his story never yet wrote down. 'Twould fill a middlin' shelf with books were it all set down way it should. Aye cod, even his trek out o' Egypt after savin' his people'd make a greater tale than ary book that clutters the shelves today. Forty years in the wilderness they spent, livin' off the country, long 'fore trap or gun was thought of, too. Fancy that. Oh not even them that wrote down the Book itself could put down aught but a smidgin of what Moses seen an' went through."

"They purely lacked the words, most like," Ma said. She sighed and clucked her lips. "But I'll declare right now, a body has to weed out a chapter right careful, even in the Good Book, 'tis that full of strollops an' Jezebels an' low goings-on. Had I read what we heard tonight in mixed company, I'd reely have swounded with shame."

"Happen it's that mixed a company, Liddy, we'll stick to the Psalms," Cam laughed.

Bucky sat listening, entranced, his spirit wandering far as he followed the deeds of these mighty characters through the realm of bold antiquity. It was a great, glorious, heroic world this, in which his mind was privileged to roam. He thought now of his own given name of Jude and came out abruptly with a question that had worried him long:

"How come I was named for the worst scutter in the whole Book, Pa? I never could figure it."

Both Cam's head and Ma's came round, mildly startled. Then a host of tiny wrinkles played about Cam's dark eyes as he closed the Book.

" 'Twant Judas you was named for, son," he chuckled. " 'Twas just plain Jude. Good enough name for ary man."

Ma put the Bible back on its shelf and blew out the light.

In the dimness of the firelight Bucky heard his father muttering to himself: "Names! Pack o' nonsense, these days. Why the sorriest man we know bears the name o' Paul. Another one's Solomon. Ol' Sol Middleton. Neither of 'em fit to lug guts to a bear."

Bucky climbed the loft ladder to his bunk, thinking on these things: of skinny old Paul Pennix, the banker, and Sol Middleton, and old King Solomon with a house full of hussies, and he thought about them all next day as he went his lonely rounds.

PROPERTY OF
FRANKFORT SCHUYLER CENTRAL
HIGH SCHOOL LIBRARY
FRANKFORT, NEW YORK   13340

13 ~~~~~~~~~~~~~~~~~~

THROUGH THE TREBLE-WELTED SHADOWS OF A SPRUCE
wood Bucky moved with silent tread, Pa's rifle held
ready-cocked in the crook of his arm. Ducking beneath
the low branches of the spruce, stopping often stone-still
to peer and listen, he was like an indistinguishable part
of the hushed winter landscape. He was following fresh
deer tracks in the deep snow. After a time he came to a
halt beneath the tentlike droop of a spruce bough and
crouched there waiting, watching the open places
among the trees ahead, where the snow lay blue-white
against the shadows. So still he was that a horned owl,
abroad by day in these dusky woods, banked air ten
feet in front of him in fright, snapping its hooked beak
with a sound like cracking nuts.

Time passed. The snow ahead got bluer with shadows. Gradually, among the far trees, three dun spots
moved falteringly, stopped and moved again. Bucky
slipped a hand out of a mitten, aimed, and squeezed
the trigger.

Pa's rifle roared and blazed. Snow bank and forest

wall bandied its echo back and forth. Two of the spots ahead whisked from sight like blown leaves.

It was a good shot. Bucky feared a bad, for two years before he and Cam had once failed to kill a deer outright and its eyes still haunted him. Now, as he ducked beneath hanging boughs into the clearing, he found a fat buck lying as if fallen asleep.

"Never knowed what hit you." Bucky drew a long breath of relief. "All right, ol' buck."

He and Cam rarely shot deer and then only for actual need. This one was to serve as the Calloways' Christmas dinner. Bucky waited for a space in complete silence. Cam never failed to do this after taking a life. It was an instinctive ritual of a natural mystic. Paradoxically, Cam always hated to take life, though he was a hunter born.

Leaning his rifle against a tree Bucky drew skinning knife and fell to work. Day was ending and it was very cold, so the job was troublesome, but he worked carefully, lifting the skin before it could freeze. Then he cut up the carcass, strung the forepart on a high limb, and with the hide and hindquarters slung over his back turned homeward. Plenty of meat now for the great day.

That evening Cam and Bucky held counsel and decided to pull all traps along the line till after Christmas.

"I'd not like to think of ary beast lyin' in trap o' mine tomorrow night," Cam said. "The trapper that won't give over an' call a truce come Christmas Day is a sorry scutter."

So Bucky set out next morning to cover the line. But first, he decided, he'd go round by the Mellott cabin to see what was toward. Two weeks gone he had bought Mrs. Mellott some buckram and a length of lining to finish Ma's cape. Ever since she and Bridie too had been working on it like beavers.

It was old Grammer Bates who answered Bucky's knock today.

"So it's you; come in then," she said with a humph and a sniff. Most folk were reared back on their dew claws at Grammer Bates' look and manner and Bucky was no exception, for Grammer, he knew, was one who shared the town's opinion of the Calloways in general. She looked at him with her hard old eyes and bade him sit.

A coffee-coolin' caution was Grammer, though well over eighty, different from all other folk, for by mere passage of time she had come into prestige and clan authority in the region as the widow of old Abner Bates, first settler on the Swiftwater. Abner had come into the country in the seventies with nothing to start with but Grammer and a pack of bear hounds. The Mellotts were purely like a nest of chicken hawks who'd found an old falcon in their midst with Grammer Bates around.

Even back in the days when Bridie and Bucky had been most together, Grammer had held a Gibraltar against him. Lately it had increased, for Bridie would soon be coming of age and there was neither name nor money nor visible means of livelihood to speak for Bucky as a possible suitor.

Mrs. Mellott bustled in, snipping a thread between sharp white teeth.

"'Twill be finished by tomorrow, Bucky," she said, "and it's a cape fit for a wedding or a coronation, if I do say so. There's not a woman from here to Poke o' Moonshine'll not be envyin' your mom when she puts it on."

She brought it out for him to see—a billowing armful that shone on the surface and glowed softly underneath. Bucky could call for it Christmas morning, she said.

But Bridie was there and said she'd fetch it over. Nothing would do but she must try it on for Bucky and pirouette round the floor. She sat down beside him finally, stroking the grain of the cape.

"I just love a beautiful furpiece," she breathed. "One of these days I'm going to have a fine coat of mink or fisher. I may go south to one of the big schools later, Mom says, and that's when I'd want it. I don't intend to stay in Swiftwater all my life."

Before Bucky rightly knew it she'd worked under his shell, like, and there he was all flushed and flustered and sort of fighting for air like a stuck sturgeon, all his stolidness fled like the wild birds in fall. For Bridie was all changed again, though 'twas only a fortnight gone that he'd seen her last. A new person each meeting. Today she made him think more than a little of Ma, with her craving for things and other places.

She was all pranked up in a flowered dress, with silk stockings and high-heel shoes. She'd a new way of looking at a man, turning her head so that she glanced over a shoulder, or even under an arm if she happened to be stooping for a chunk of firewood or such. She'd a way of laughing, too—no longer the girlish giggle he knew, but a bright and limpid thing, like clear water sliding over a fall. A fellow had no sooner got hold of his solemnness than she'd broken it down for him again. She looked a downright lady and for the life of him Bucky couldn't drag up aught to say, and his weeks in the deep woods helped none there. He went weak and helpless as a timber wolf with a galena pill in his lights and scarce heard what the women were saying, he was so busy watching her.

They'd all heard of his fight with the woods devil. They plied him with a dozen questions, but he could prize up nothing to tell them beyond a yea or a nay. Grammer Bates was a mite of help there. She knew a deal about trapping and she related a tale or two of the old days. Bucky didn't even try to match it, for 'twas plain Grammer believed that trapping and hunting too had gone pindling and no-account since the days when old Abner ranged the Swiftwater woods.

He was glad to get away. Still and all there was a lorn lag to his step as he headed toward the Jackpine. He kept seeing the Mellotts' bright sitting room and Bridie in her flowered dress, babbling along like a waterfall, saying things sweet as sap. It was a caution what a difference a few ruffles made in a girl, he thought. It was a caution how muddle-minded girls could get.

Up along the silent valley he moved, springing his traps and releasing the thong-held sets. He'd be glad of a day of rest. He hadn't known how tired he was till the thought of rest had brought it out. There was but scanty catch along the line, as if the creatures themselves had set out to call a holiday. In the northwest it was thickening up. Likely it would snow for Christmas.

Three days before, Bucky had set up his spring-gun set for Fire Eyes, and a fresh-killed rabbit crouching lifelike, dead in line of the sights. He'd been proud of that set, all camouflaged with green boughs, but when he came to it now a great surprise awaited him. It was a red fox, not a panther, that had pounced upon the crouching rabbit. There he lay stone-dead, with a bullet through his head, a rarer catch as far as value went than two or three of Fire Eyes' kind. A trapper's prize. What would Cam say to that, he wondered, as he took down the old Sharps.

Twenty minutes more and he came to the water set he'd made at the foxes' drinking place. There he stood bemazed. For 'twas old Fire Eyes himself who'd elected to drink there, with his forefeet on the snow-capped rock. There were his big pug marks in the snow. But a fox trap was never meant to hold such as he. He'd gone away from there in crazy bounds, taking trap, chain, and clog with him.

Bucky followed the addled trail and five hundred yards away he came upon the bloodstained trap, torn off a forefoot by main strength and still holding a mouthful of panther fur in its tight-closed teeth. From now on old Fire Eyes would take a deal of catching indeed.

This day had been full of turnover and surprise. Who'd ever have expected a plan of Cam's to miscarry? It all went to show the strange way things had of working around.

14 ~~~~~~~~~~~~

*H*ABIT HAD BUCKY UP AS USUAL AT DAWN NEXT
morning. The night had been windless and a light snow
had fallen, as if specially ordered, frosting every twig
and needle in the pinewoods with a glint as of fairy se-
quins. It had laid a hush over all the land.

Bucky felt prime and superfine as he built up the
hearth fire. Today he was the man of the place indeed
and Santa Claus in the bargain. A week gone he'd
bought dishes and a playhouse for Viney down in town.
For Cam he'd gotten a fine new pipe and a pound of the
best of Stemline's crimp cut. He had it stowed in the
storehouse. Ma would soon have her cape. There'd be
nothing for him though, for no one would have gotten in
to town. He'd just keep busy round the place and carry
it off as if nothing like that mattered, but it wouldn't be
easy. Already he felt a sort of lump in his throat, just
thinking about it.

Last night Ma had baked a fruitcake in the big Dutch
oven. All night deermeat had been simmering over the
fire. Bucky, his face glowing from its cold-water scrub-

bing, managed a wink at Cam over Ma's shoulder. Later
he grinned at Ma when Viney wasn't looking.

The family had scarce finished cakes and bacon when
the jangle of sleighbells sounded. It was the Mellott cutter plowing through the drifts of the woods road, bearing Bridie in a red tam and a plaid Mackinaw and Jeth
Mellott at the reins, just back from the lumber camp to
the north. They tarried but a minute, for they were on
their way to town. They left two crackling paper bun-
dles on the table, one light and round, the other a solid,
heavy affair.

Viney had long since set up her new house and moved
in doll and dishes and Cam's new pipe was glowing
peacefully before Cam winked and Bucky placed one of
the crackling paper packages in Ma's lap. For a space
Ma sat like a stunned one as the glowing furpiece bil-
lowed out of its wrapping. Slowly she looked round at
the family and back at the cape, then she threw her
apron over her head and sat sobbing as if in dire grief.

Bucky watched stricken and tongue-halted. Never had
he seen Ma cry. He and Cam must have botched things
somehow. Then he saw Cam's eye on her with a twinkle
in it and he sensed that Ma must be so wild glad that
nothing but tears were an out.

Cam said, "You'd a' had a fisher cape long gone,
Liddy, an' many another fancy piece, had I had my way
an' wish."

Ma wiped her eyes at last and sat looking down at the
gleaming furs, stroking them with reverent hand.

"All them lovely skins," she said. "Worth more'n this
whole house, an' the land too, most like. Oh it ain't
right, Cam. Doane Shattuck had ought to had these in
payment. 'Twould a' purely cleared our slate with him."

There was a shaft of logic there, but Cam carried it
off with a chuckle.

"Ol' Shattuck ain't took to wearin' fancy capes yet,

Liddy. Now let's us not fret an' figger, a day like this. Shattuck'll git his money in time an' he knows it. We'll pay off all debts, by little by."

"Shuh. We're like to be takin' double catch from now on, Ma," Bucky put in largely. "Pa'll soon be helpin' again."

"That's right. Come now, Liddy. Least you can do is to see do it fit."

A thing done and sealed was naught to be mooned over. Soon Ma stood before the square of wall mirror in cape and gloves and her feathered hat, her eyes gone contented and bright as a girl's.

"It don't go proper with this old skirt," she said, "but I'll walk off for you."

She walked off while the family admired. Viney sighed in wonder and Bucky just sat gazing. He'd purely forgotten about his own Christmas.

"It's right smart round the shoulders. Sets you off pretty as a queen on a playin' card," Cam cried. "You don't look a day over twenty-five, I'll swear. Was I up on my feet I'd steal a bait o' kisses an' a hug or two."

Ma came over glowing and bent to give her man a hearty smack. Cam let out a wild Indian yell. It was a long time before Ma could shed her cape and settle down to cooking.

"It's been a sorry time since I been out o' this place," she said. "Townfolk have benoyed an' benastied us so long I never cared which nor whether about them an' their doin's, but now I purely aim to go to some. Next week I'll bribe Doc Waters to fetch me in his rig some afternoon."

Bucky had begun to oil some traps like a staid old man when he heard Viney's penetrant whisper; then Cam's quiet voice jerked him up.

"Well, son, looks like there's another packet lyin' yonder, last o' the lot. Reckon it belongs to be yours."

Cam lay smiling. Viney brought the package to Bucky—the heavy, hard one the Mellotts had left on the table. Bucky had sluffed all thought of presents from his mind, but now the lump was back in his throat as he fumbled with wrappings. Oh he knew what it was long before he brought the thing to light—gleaming blue-steel barrel, polished walnut stock—a high-powered Springfield rifle, brand spanking new and giving off the rousing scent of new steel and gunsmith's oil. A lifetime thing.

Vaguely he heard Ma's voice telling how Viney had struggled through the drifts to town, carrying skins to trade for it, how Nat Stemline had delivered it to the Mellotts' for secret keeping till the great day. It was more than he could bear. The hot tears ran down his cheeks.

" 'Twas a grain cruel to keep you lingerin' thataway, son," came Cam's voice, full of understanding, "but I wanted to see could you take it like a man, with the rest of us dithering about our gifts. You done right noble."

The next half hour was one Bucky would always remember. Getting the heft and feel and balance of the new gun, the cool caress of it on hand and cheek, studying its shiny bore and the magic of its mechanism, sighting on distant pinetops.

"You should a' had it long gone," Cam said, "for the way you handled all since I been down. You can try her out come afternoon. Happen you'd like to own mine better, you can have that in its place."

"Oh, Pa!" The words came in a gasp. "It's the old curly maple I'd choose, if it's all one to you." Cam's rifle was like Cam's self. Around it clung an eight-year saga of epic hunting, far travel, and adventure experienced by Cam.

"Then the old 'un's yours," Cam said, moved. He

turned under his blankets and chuckled. "That way we'm both drawin' a present out of it."

Ma's dinner was plenteous—a whole leg of roast venison and all the trimmings, including deer heart and liver. Ma cooked her venison with thin strips of salt pork and stuffed it with cloves of garlic for seasoning. As always, tender browned wild rice went with the meat, and a relish of wild-gooseberry jam.

The family had not nearly finished eating when there came a subdued rap. Peter Nigosh stood without when Bucky opened.

"Come in, set down, Nigosh," Cam called out heartily. "There's abundance here."

With a grunt of greeting the Indian came in and took a chair at the table, dropping his fur cap on the floor. Without ado he took the food set before him and began devouring twice as much as any of his hosts.

"Deer liver," he said once, smacking his lips. "Pooty good."

Thereafter he said no word, simply ate prodigiously. His silence carried no lack of amity to Cam and Bucky. But Ma fidgeted. Long after the family had finished the Indian continued eating in silence, helping himself when no one else would. No telling how long it might have gone on had not Ma finally removed what was left of the roast.

Nigosh wiped his mouth with the back of his hand and belched with satisfaction. He sat on for a space, running his tongue around his teeth, and sometimes a finger. He and Cam exchanged a few remarks in Micmac. Nigosh's black, obsidian eyes seemed to be studying the air and the ceiling poles.

"I see a dream on your face," he said, looking briefly at Cam. "It is on the right."

Cam nodded. "I know the dream. 'Tis the dream of a hawk."

"Then I was told true," murmured Nigosh. "A hawk dream must be dreamed out. It must be kept good. Mm. Yeah."

Cam lay waiting with diffidence, for long since he had learned respect for the Micmac old men and their dream telling. But there was another long silence, except for Ma bustling about her cleaning up. Nigosh asked at length:

"You see my brother anywhere, t'late?"

"Jacques? No, nary hide nor hair, but I been bedrid a long spell."

"Been long gone. Too long fer drunk, we think. Mebbe dead."

He arose and took up his cap. At the door he turned and said in formal Micmac idiom, "Friend of mine," and was gone.

"Eat an' run," Ma sniffed. Her mouth had gone sewed-up and hard. "Whoo!" she cried disgustedly. "The place'll have to be aired clean through for a spell, cold as it is, after that feller steamin' by the fire." She flung open the door and flapped her apron in the air.

"Nigosh is a good friend," Cam said defensively. "Many's a meal I've had at his lodge, or stayed the night."

"You could a' done better than stay with the likes of him," Ma said. "He wants his needin's, your friend, an' a good bath besides."

"The Injun way ain't ours," Cam said, "but there's a mort o' things they could teach us for all that. Now I never see Nigosh but there's a thing or two he knows that I don't, an' he'm able to tell it. That's more'n I could say for ary white man. Like that dream o' mine. Two nights going I dreamed of a hawk, a-swoopin' an' stabbin' at all around. Nigosh saw it on me. There's no better dream teller among the Micmacs than him. He's a born farseer, too."

"Bosh an' moonshine," Ma flared. "Wish he'd see how far he can keep from my fire from now on, that's all."

But the rest of the afternoon was a happy time. Cam and Ma both told stories of Christmas doings they'd known in times past. Ma sang an old song or two—the one Viney loved about a zanie girl called Lattledy Lal. It ran on and on in endless verses, ending with:

> Lal, Lal, Lattledy Lal,
> Oh, Lattledy, Lattledy, Lal, Lal, Lal.

And another about a drowning when Ma was a girl back in York State:

> The ice being broken,
> They both tumbled in;
> George Betsey got drowned,
> Billy Lindsey could swim.

Then nothing would do for Bucky but that Cam sing a bit of "High Chin Bob"—Bucky's favorite hero. It told through many bars of balladry how High Chin roped him a great panther in a wild canyon. Unable to drag the panther to death, Bob would bedogged if he'd loose him, so cat, horse, and rider swept down the mountain till all were dashed to death and ever after men had seen them pass on starlit nights, still roped together and sweeping like the wind.

The Calloways were to have still another visitor before the day was done. Toward dusk they heard the sound of sleighbells again and across the woodlot old Doc Waters came stumping toward the cabin. He carried something under his arm which he plunked down by the door as he took off his greatcoat. A shiny yellow crutch!

"Just thought this would be a good day for the unveilin', Cam," Doc chuckled as he bent over Cam's bandaged leg. " 'Twas due most any day now and I couldn't think up a good excuse why it shouldn't be Christmas. The quicker you start crutch-movin' now the quicker you'll shed crutch and splint and step out on your own again."

"I'll be John-dogged!" Cam cried. "A body'll soon be able to sight the end o' this business, I do believe!"

"Two weeks on the crutch, moving about a good bit every day, then you'll be able to ease some weight on the leg, a bit at a time," Doc said.

A bit later, Cam, weak from bed-lying, but jubilant, was hobbling about the cabin with the aid of the crutch, peering curiously from door and window at a landscape he'd not set eyes on in weeks. And that evening he sat in his leather chair by the hearth instead of taking to his bed again, his bandaged leg stretched out before him. On the table glowed the Radiant Beam, washing the walls in gold, and there was another special reading from the Book in celebration.

Oh, it *had* been a day.

15

By JANUARY BUCKY HAD TO MAKE HIS TRAP ROUNDS BY snowshoe, except for stretches where the wind had scoured the drifts away. Two days now it took him to cover his line and so every third night he had to make snow camp in the deep woods, far up near the head of the Jackpine, sleeping in the bark-covered, half-faced lean-to he and Cam had set up in the fall.

The first few times he took old Sounder with him and the two of them huddled for warmth beneath the blankets, facing the small fire Bucky set going. But as Cam had always said, a dog made a difference in the woods, and soon Bucky left him at home. He didn't need him for warmth or protection, and it got so he wanted nothing to break the spell of the silence that went with it all like a deep current. Besides, the old dog wanted none of it. He had a civilized scorn for such primitive huddling in the snow round a smidgin of fire when there was a cabin warm and windproof for the taking. He had a healthy fear of the night dogs, too. Many a time he had lain listening to the terrible voice of the wolf pack threatening to take him back to the olden wild he had left, via the digestive system if he'd not come otherwise.

Without the dog Bucky saw and felt all the things he longed to know. The deep woods were showing him their secret face now, their winter side, which few men ever have the need, or the hardihood, to learn. Almost too much to bear it was at first, that deathly, diamond stillness, that awesome and categorical presence. The thick spruce silence was more than silence; it was a spell. There were caves of stillness in this valley that seemed never to have been stirred since time began. The whole of Bucky's being was shrunk to a hard tight knot in its stand against the tremendous suck and onslaught of the cold, the black night, and the loneliness. Only because he was timber-bred did he grow accustomed to it.

All around him, tranced and white as a hooded secret, crowded the woods, making not a move, yet beckoning, communing with him. Just the feel of them went through and over him like nothing else in the world. The same fearsome trees that had furtively crowded him in the fall as if they hated to see him getting out of their clutches, were opening to him now.

Something in him knew the woods and the woods knew him. There was a knowledge between them and he could hear them calling to him. Oh, he'd heard that elfin-horn note long before, back in fall when the trees first turned with frost fire, and even the fall before, though mighty faint it had been and not to be read by him. Sweeter than a hound dog running a fox was that call, but subtle as a floating filament of spider web, thin and bittersweet as grief. Not meant for every ear, that horn note that calls only to the hunter-born.

Now the dark conifers stood quiet, listening, as if they were tranced. They talked softly among themselves in winter tones, all round the lean-to where Bucky lay.

The tall firs with their high heads together whispered, the ancient matted hemlocks muttered low, like so many hoary sages worrying over the flightiness or lax morals of the community. Sometimes they sighed. The mightiest one, fifteen feet in circumference, would start it. Then his neighbors would sigh. Two younger trees, which had fallen into the arms of their sires in some long-ago storm, would rub against them fifty feet up and murmur "Ah-men."

There was none of the lighthearted murmur a body heard in summertime, from the water trees when their many leaves were dancing in the sunlight—the flippant young ash and beech, the flagrant vine maples and timid, girlish willows, not above gossiping, ridiculing the noble pines and firs, pretending they could not understand their subdued, sere talk from the north. They set great stock in their own svelte beauty, did the water trees, but they were envious underneath, you could lay to that.

Around the night camp, life in all its olden meanings held forth. But you had to love the wild things to their very bones to take in the things Bucky was learning now.

He had become almost immune to the cold; he knew when to keep moving, how best to move to keep the cold from eating in, how to take shelter in snow, in case the cut of the wind became unbearable. His heavy felt boots kept his feet free of frostbite at all times. No cold could penetrate the devilskin cap Ma had made, with its pull-down flaps for neck and ears. He'd heavy mittens of the same skin that he could slough off, with gloves beneath for the handling of his traps. His snow camp was no longer a boogerish place of gloom and dread, but a place he loved. Snow had banked high and hard around and over it on three sides, keeping out all wind. Oh it was a wonderful thing, snow, for holding the frost at bay; it took the stuff of cold to fight cold on its own ground.

He didn't even light a fire now of a night out. He begrudged driving back the spirits of the place even that much. So he went without coffee, ate a cold snack from his knapsack, lay down in his wickiup, head toward the opening, Pa's rifle handy beside him. On moonlit nights, he saw the spectral ranks of the snowshoe rabbits hopping along their well-worn trails toward their willow gnaws by the stream banks, led by a big and wary buck, all silent and white as the snow itself. Now and again he saw a weasel tracking the rabbits and heard the thin, far scream of the trail's end. He'd pick one rabbit, a weasel would, and hang to that trail alone like grim death till fear finally froze the rabbit in its running and the killer fastened to its warm and pulsing throat.

Far sounds brought to his ears a hundred wild tales. He saw the great owls coasting silent as death angels over the soft moonlit tips of the firs, to swoop suddenly down and take their tithe from the rabbits' flitting ranks. And often he saw a file of a score of rabbits stop stonestill and crouch transfixed at the distant booming of the horned owl, that hollow, ventriloquial note that penetrated all the woods at once without hint of direction, warning that death was on the wing.

Once he saw the death battle of two earless snowy owls, accompanied by a hissing and snapping and by jagged cries, as if a pair of witch-hags were having a set-to. It went on till the great, hooked claw of one fighter closed over the other's head, piercing eyes and brain, and the vanquished one swung head down and pendant for a space, then dropped stone-dead to the snow. What devil's business was back of that battle there was no telling. The victor yelped like a mad one, but did not touch the fallen body, simply floated away.

The moonless nights were quite another thing. In the blackness all manner of eyes flitted, green, or burning red and low to the ground—which meant the weasel clan. Always they were in pairs, always two by two. The whole night was eyes. The stars in the vast blue-black sky blinked with them. And there, too, they seemed always to blink in pairs.

At first the timber wolves came round the lean-to, their yellow-green eyes weaving in and out, but after Bucky shot three of them they came no more. He and Cam had no scruple about thinning out the ranks of this ravening horde from the north, who spent their days and nights killing the game and raiding the settlers' stock. Once Bucky shot a prowling lynx.

Oh, it got so he begrudged sleep and drowsed but fitfully, like an animal, in his eagerness to miss as little as could be of the nightly pageant. One of these nights old Fire Eyes himself might come prowling round the lean-to. He'd know him right enough, by his big green night-lamps.

One day on a side trip up a valley, he found the big winter yarding place of the Swiftwater deer herds. There were three big connecting yards in this secret retreat, tramped out by many hoofs beneath the overhanging branches of the evergreens, with plenty of territory round about for extending the yards if feeding grew scarce. The yard walls were straight and four feet high, hardened by alternate freezing and melting. High ridges round about protected the place from the force of prevailing storms. Round the yard edges were the tracks of wolves and foxes and the broad round marks of hungry bobcats.

The leading bucks of the herd snoofed warningly at

sight of him. They came forward shaking their heads in defiance. They were lean and awkward-looking, shorn of their summer antlers. They remained wary, but after a time they ceased to snort their challenges, accepting the boy standing among the trees with equanimity, for on them was the magic truce of winter.

Bucky thought about old Lophorn, the lone moose bull. Moose yarded up for winter. Did Lophorn too winter along the Swiftwater, or did he light a rag for distant parts before snow came? No one knew, but Bucky didn't think so. Every spare hour now he made side trips in the woods searching. He went along the valleys where the trees were thick and finally one late, dark afternoon his quest was answered.

He was about to turn back to his camp when, parting the thick evergreen branches to peer ahead, he saw it. In the narrowing throat-latch of the valley's head old Lophorn had tramped himself out a long yard that ran a hundred yards or more upward between two toes of old Sugarloaf's base. There stood the gaunt dark bull, somber and sad-looking without his antlers, and beyond him stood two cows, an old and a young! Bucky's heart thudded beneath his breastbone. The Red Gods had been good to the lonely bull the fall before; he had achieved a mating in his chosen country, had Lophorn, and by spring a moose calf or two would be dropped, the beginning of a herd along the Swiftwater if all went well. The thing Cam had always hoped for.

There came a vast whooshing sound, as old Lophorn saw him and came forward, his little eyes red. Over nine feet tall he stood at his humped shoulder, dark, vast, and uncouth. Bucky did not even tarry to whet the old bull's temper. Quietly he slipped away, and as he went he wove in his mind a magic ring-pass-not round Lophorn, a circle of protection that none might penetrate.

He'd breathe no word of this to any but Cam till spring thaw came.

Yes, these were the days and nights that marked his initiation into the cult of finished woodsmen. Apotheosis of all his years in the Swiftwater woods.

16 ～～～～～～～～

$\mathcal{A}$LF SIMES WAS DYING TO TUCK THE HEARTY SOUND of human voice and laughter in his ear and cradle it there for a spell. Just to swap a string of words with someone, no matter who all. Lord of the Jay Birds, if he could but sit down across table, stump, or grocery counter for half an hour, say, and talk, even just clap-clap with a coffee-coolin' schoolmarm—that was all Alf asked! Let her wind up proper and tell all till she run down, then he'd ask her about it all over again. Alf was dying to hear his own voice.

It was hard wintering it alone in the deep woods for one born with the silver tongue. In usual course a few men stopped by Alf's place even in midwinter, and if there was any news shaking Alf had it before the sediment settled. But not this year. The snow and cold had broken all records. Ever since the first snow Alf had been holed up playing it solitaire. He wasn't built for the likes of this.

In winter Alf hadn't even his hired man to talk to. Hen Pine came over but once a day for the choring. Alf would lie in wait for him, but old Hen would come at odd hours, or after dark, and usually slip away unseen. Lately Alf's son rarely stopped by. When he did it was no powwow, for Hance was as mum as Alf was loquacious. He'd stored up a sight of grist for his mill, Alf had; more than he could rightly contain. Most any day a body might have heard him declaiming to his bare walls. An almighty waste of good spit, that was.

One cold day in February Alf snubbed himself short in one of these vocal perorations.

"You'll be blattin' to yourself like a sheep-herdin' coot if ye don't get out o' here an' see some'un soon," he told himself.

He thought of his son's cabin, but Hance's wife and he were at swords' points. Alf had not set foot in her house for over a year, to the delight of young Mrs. Simes, who warmly returned the slight. Then he recalled hearing that Cam Calloway was laid up.

Alf came to his feet with a blasphemous resolution. Cam's cabin was over two miles away. It would be a mortal chore getting through the drifts for an old man of seventy. But when he got there what a day they'd make of it, by the crippled criminy! A man with a broke leg couldn't up and get away from you. They'd talk till the icicles fell off the eaves where the Lord had made 'em hang.

Alf banked his fire. He stuck some eatin' tobacco into his cheek and got into his sheepskin coat. He took up a strip of jerky to chew on along the way.

The going was hard, the drifts often waist high, and old Alf wasn't sure on his feet any more. But a cane would have been worse than useless here. Alf wasn't dressed for such weather either. His salt-and-pepper pants weren't meant for such snow, and neither were his old overshoes. They slewed him back in places a good six inches to every foot he hove forward, and he stumbled often, but he went stomping on, his gray eyes shining fiercely out of the shag of his whiskers and eyebrows. They darted hopefully here, there, and yonder, for news of another human. News of anything moving. God knew what had been brewing in the world since he'd last seen anyone. Maybe the whole country was in a close-to with this Russian peril they'd been talking of.

It was not midday when he started forth, but it was well on into afternoon before he thumped at the Calloways' door. Ma was thunderstruck as the old man hobbled in—rimed with frost from head to foot and panting. He'd fallen more than once along the way. It was a time before he could get his breath. Amazed and overawed, Cam reached for his crutch and struggled to his feet.

"I take it right kindly, your comin' all this way to see us," he said. "Liddy, draw up the big chair for Alf."

"Fiddlesticks," Alf panted. " 'Twant such a chore. Just last week I heard about your bad leg, Cam, my boy, an' says I, I'll get over there 'tween storms if it's the last thing I do."

But when Cam felt called on to tell of his accident, the old man veered him off. The open fire and the coffee Ma poured for him put the life back into him and from there on Alf himself took over. For the first fifteen minutes he said everything over twice for good measure, and the cabin rang with his machine-gun delivery. He soon began to surpass himself, for Cam had always been one of his best listeners. He talked largely of all things under heaven. Oh, he'd worked out many a new tack since fall to confound men's wits. His trickiest pack of contradictions had developed since Cam had seen him last and that was on the subject of dogs. In order to run tantamount to all precedent, Alf had cultivated a violent

antipathy to dogs and a correspondingly violent liking
for cats. A dog, Alf said, was a natural-born traitor and a
coward. Hadn't dogs gone against their kind from the
beginning? Wouldn't a dog turn thief, bully, or butcher
at a word from his master?

"Don't dogs go against all the rest of the wild? A dog
ain't even to be trusted by the friends of his owner. Like
as not he'll take the pants off them, or a chunk of leg. Let
it get past dark and he'll come snarlin' at his own master
till his nose tells him he's buckin' up again' his own
meal ticket. It's the grub he gets, first an' last, that keeps
him hangin' to your heels, an' the mollyin' he gets on
winter nights, wrigglin' an' tail waggin' his way in by
the fire, fawnin' an' finickin' with the younkers, while the
rest of the varmints lay out in the cold."

Licked up their own spittle, too, dogs did. There
wasn't another one in the whole of Noah's cargo would
do that.

"Go 'way an' leave your dog tied an' you can hear him
howlin' down in the next county. No character. Thinks
you're goin' to let him starve on the spot. No more sper-
rit than a Flathead Injun. Then take their spittin' an'
slobberin' on your hand an' clean up to your face if
you'll let 'em. And here's another thing: Let a man get
down on another man an' the first thing he calls him is a
dirty dog. Why is that? Because for a minute or so he's
got sense enough to speak the truth, that's why."

That purely raised Ma Calloway's fur, listening to such
talk with old Sounder lying right there by the fire.
She'd like to have sounded off a short piece of her own,
just there, and she came devilish near doing it too, as
Cam could see. But there was the visitor's white hair.
Cam merely chuckled. He savored the delivery rather
than the letter of Alf's talk.

"Take cats, though," Alf ran on. "They got minds of

their own. Quit feedin' 'em an' they go feed theirselves, no bones about it. An' at the same time they're a-clearin' out the rats an' other vermin about the place. They like a man from the teeth in, cats do; keep their lip to theirselves. No noise, no slobberin'. A sluice of milk now an' again that nobody misses sets 'em to singin'. Cats don't hang around the table, beggin' the truck off your plate, nor hang their jowl on your knee for notice. Glad to be shut of you when you go 'way, they are. Gives 'em a chance to think an' tend their own business."

He spoke with pride of his own twelve cats and his panther and Cam ventured to argue.

"It's mortal funny," he said. "I can't understand it. Twelve cats an' a panther around your place."

"Nothin' funny in it," old Alf bristled. "I like 'em."

"But a sneakin' catamount, comin' in an' out o' the house. It ain't natural to love a thing like that."

Alf snorted. "I got 'em all beat for somethin' to keep me company," he said. "He's house-broke, too."

"Don't you figger it's sort o' flyin' in the face o' Providence like, sleepin' with him comin' in an' out?"

"No more'n sleepin' with a dog in the house. An' he ain't no dog, thank God!"

"Someday he'm apt to climb up on somethin' an' drop on your neck."

"He don't do no climbin'," snorted Alf. "He ain't been taught to. But if he did, he'd get tunneled. Don't think I'd sit by seein' him get wild an' stand for it."

When darkness came old Alf was just warmed up. Soon Bucky came in from his long day on the line and Alf pricked up and started afresh. He gave them tall trapping tales. He advised them how to run their line better, from A to Izzard. You'd have thought he was the original pioneer on the Swiftwater, who'd tamed the howling wilderness down till weaker folk could dwell here.

He gave no sign of going, as any could see, so Ma set out the evening meal. Supper was a two-hour affair. Old Alf pecked and dabbled with his food, now and again taking a small bite, which would not interrupt the flow of rhetoric.

Late evening had come and the night dogs were howling before their visitor made ready to depart. And then there was nothing for it but Bucky, after his long day in the woods, must get out the lantern and accompany him. Old Alf protested, but you could see he looked on it as his just due. Alf shouted parting shots at the open cabin door as long as he was in hail.

Bucky preceded him with the lantern along the dark road. He had snowshoes with him and where the going was heavy he beat down a passage for Alf to follow in. That left Alf with breath enough for fresh discourse and he kept up a rapid-fire monologue as they tramped. Alf had a new project in mind for the coming spring. He was going to raise black fox on his back woodlot. As soon as ever the frost was out of the ground he'd put in some strong wire pens. He'd start out with a single pair and by the time another winter came he'd have prime fox fur to sell when the market was high.

Bucky timidly brought forth his plan for a wild-goose sanctuary. He was amazed to have the old man pounce on it like a fish hawk on a shallowed pickerel. 'Twas the best idea he'd heard of in a scad of years. Why a wild-bird sanctuary would be a blessing for everyone, not only for the geese. Alf craved to hear all the details and he pumped Bucky with questions all the rest of the way home.

" 'Course, the town's a-goin' to benasty you an' do things round the corner to stop you," Alf said when at

last they arrived at his doorstep. "Swiftwater an' the
tourists think of nothin' but shootin' when they see a
wild goose. But just you go ahead with your idea, son,
an' pay 'em no mind. It could just be I can help you out
a mite, when the time comes round. I'll pointedly try
to, my boy, yes, I'll pointedly try. Good night. Good
night. An' don't forget Alf Simes is goin' to stand right
back of you."

Alf went stumping into the house, laughing to himself. Bucky could hear him laughing even after the door
had been closed. He turned homeward with a deep new
elation.

Going back, Bucky put out the lantern to conserve its
precious oil. He took the road that led past the Mellott
cabin. Here there were fresh sleigh tracks in the recent
snow. The Mellott living room was brightly lighted as
usual and a cutter stood waiting by the porch, with a
restless mare ruckling and stamping in the shafts. The
Mellotts had company too.

A sudden whelming loneliness made Bucky veer aside
through the trees to get a brief glimpse of that cheerful,
lighted room. He paused beneath a pine. There sat Mrs.
Mellott bent over her eternal piecing. Bridie was moving about in the lamplight, laughing, all pranked out
in her ruffled dress. Something to look at through any
window, night or day, was Bridie now. Then Bucky saw
who the "company" was. Whit Turner sat on the other
side of the fireplace, arrayed in new store clothes tonight and showing off with tricks and banter and mild
sparking. Quite a man Whit had become in the past few
months, all legs and torso and rangy arms. And Bridie
sat there liking it all, as you could see.

Sore as a baited badger, Bucky was off down the road
toward home with long, anger-driven stride. Then he

remembered his lantern, which he'd set down for a moment in the snow, and had to go creeping back for it.

There was a hot spot in his chest that didn't cool down all that night, nor did it let him sleep except in troubled snatches.

17 ~~~~~~~~~~~~~~

*M*ARCH WAS A WHOLE PUSH OF RAW, BOISTEROUS weather that came raiding down from the north, cold almost as January. There hadn't been a speculation stirring that year, even among the old-timers, about Ground Hog Day. For not a ground hog living would have been fool enough to claw his way out through ice and snow at any time in February to see whether he cast shadow or no.

Cam had never held with ground-hog signs. It was a tale dreamed up by old women, he claimed. The bear was the real barometer. When you saw the first bear sign you knew winter'd really broken and spring had turned the corner. Anyone could tell by the way Keg slept on that a good stretch of winter still lay ahead.

Furs remained prime and the Calloways and the deep woods toiled on together through the favoring season and the valley more than lived up to its fall promise. Prime fur, more than they'd ever known before, was piled in the storehouse, for Cam had been working with Bucky again for two weeks past, still a bit slow on the trail, but able to cover the line twice a week, so that

Bucky could trap up the more inaccessible side valleys.

That spring should have been a time of triumph and harvest, of measuring up the rich woods toll in piles and bales and packing it off to trade for the best in victuals and many an extra-fancy thing to put on the back or brighten the house. Certainly the Calloways' catch would be cause for seven-day wonder this year, as far as quantity and variety went. But not in value. Things had gone awry in the fur trade, in the unexpected way an ax will slip and maim at times for all a woodsman's care.

A long arm of the Hudson's Bay Company, that great organization that dealt in fur and death, had stretched out that winter to include the Swiftwater country in its empire. Word of it had come in January. A great new trading post was being built only fifty miles to the east of Swiftwater. French Canadian *voyageurs* and strange Indians had begun drifting into town. Many of them brought pelts. These were the free traders. But the great company with its army of trappers was against all free trade, all competition. It saw to it that the price of furs was cut almost in half—just in time to leave the Calloways shorn of their hard-earned profits.

It was well on in February when Bucky first learned of this. He hadn't rightly believed it, in spite of the pitifully small bait of victuals and a strip of cloth he'd gotten for a prime otter skin. It was all due to some rumor. Nat Stemline thought so too. But the low price continued. Pressure was being put on Nat to make him turn his store into a branch post for the company.

Bucky didn't tell Cam. It was March before Cam learned the truth. Bucky had never seen him go so dark.

There comes a time when misfortune sickens men. But Cam held his bitter words in. He wouldn't speak of it. At first he had wanted to take their catch south to the big towns and try to sell it for more, but after much figuring it became plain they'd lose what profit was in it in the cost.

All through March they kept the secret to themselves. With the first thaw they pulled all traps and packed their plunder in to Stemline's store, to sell for what it would bring. Cam was not one to haggle. They settled for three hundred and fifty dollars and a bit of credit at the store for a catch on which they'd hoped for more than a thousand. They owed more than the three hundred and fifty to Doane Shattuck on their timber land.

Cam, leaning on the counter, looked at the date as Nat Stemline entered it carefully in his big book— *April 1st.*

"The Day o' the Fool," he said with a wry grimace. "Aye, we chose the date well."

Days afterward Cam's spirits had still not risen. Bucky, too, did much thinking about this turnover, which all overnight had undermined the safe surety of their old life—his and Cam's. But as mild weather set in he could scarce bear in mind such things, with the song of the south wind in the woods and the feel of it in his veins. Not for anything the world could give would he have foregone his wonderful winter on the trap line, those greatest months of his life. He had been growing phenomenally outside as well, and was beginning to thicken out. His muscles stretched as flexibly as vines filled with sap. Oh, there was a prodigal strength and ebullience in him now that there was time to rest a mite, like a stream released from winter's clamp. A few more months and he'd be nudging six feet high.

Meantime spring had come brazening through the hills like a switch-hippedy habitant girl on a full day off. All overnight the hills began weeping freshets and near and far came the soft, sucking *chug* of collapsing snowbanks. The Little Jackpine sang roisterous songs as it came forty-nining down from old Sugarloaf.

123

Before the snow had rightly melted catskins were swelling along the waterways and green spears of wild flag and Johnny-jump-up were piercing the wet earth. Another few days and popple and birch were in bud, snakes were coming out of their hidey-holes, and cricket-frogs were tuning it up in the shadowy places. Everything in a mighty hurry after the long dark. Old Earth was great with her children, bulb and grub, seed and toad and sleepy mammal, to say nothing of talky little newborn rivulets.

Cam took note of all with quiet omniscience.

"The geese'll not stop this spring," he announced one day at dinner.

Bucky's face fell. "How can you tell so certain sure, Pa?"

Cam bent his head, reflecting. "It's that kind of spring," he said. "You can smell it in the air. It ain't only spring here; it's spring clean up beyond Hudson's Bay. Ol' Winter was grim an' long, but when his back broke he was dead for keeps. Most years the geese'll foller the rag edge o' spring on north to their feedin' grounds up in the sphagnum swamps. But this spring it's a straightaway race for the north an' they'll not even come in gun range of us."

It was that evening at sunset that the first clanging hosts of the geese crossed the sky. And it was as Cam had said; they flew high and very fast, their long necks stretched out tenuously to the north, where lush feeding awaited them at their nesting place beyond Hudson's Bay.

This was the time when Cam and Bucky made their yearly trip up the slopes of old Sugarloaf to dig for sang root to sell in town for the drug trade. This climb was always a pilgrimage, important almost as the first fall hunting. They spent a full day at it the first week of April. They brought out a great bag of sang, and another filled with boneset, which was good for fever, and dittany and pipsissewa, which were used for medicinal tea to purify the blood. Always there was a ready market for these at Stemline's store.

It was sunset when they arrived in the clearing with their sacks. They found Ma and Viney standing in the wood lot, watching the weirdest-looking animal Bucky had yet seen. It turned out it was nothing but Keg, who had just emerged from his long hideout in the root cellar. He was scarce awake yet. A body would never have recognized him and by the look he didn't rightly know himself. For he'd gone to sleep fat as a butter ball and come out lean as any specter. Yes, he'd gone to sleep four months before as a mere stripling and had slept himself into man's estate.

He had grown many inches over all, but mostly 'twas in his legs and feet. His head and sides were gaunt and fallen in. There was a woebegone look about him and he wanted something mightily, but 'twas nothing that humans could give him. Ma had set out a pan of scraps for him, but he'd spurned it, upsetting it with his nose, and now he was hunkered down in the midst of it, his head swaying disconsolately from side to side. His eyes were glazed with the spring sickness of his kind.

"Oh, ain't he the sorry somethin'?" Cam said, setting down his bag.

Keg loosed a bawl of angry irritation and abruptly whirled about, teeth bared in defiance. He'd thought for an instant that a grown bear had crept up on him. And a grown bear had. His growl had been fierce as the Middle-Sized Bear and the Great Big Bear rolled into one and never again would he know the aimless play of cubhood.

Cam laughed long and loud, the first deep laugh Bucky had heard from him since his accident back in the fall. Keg, with the look of one piqued and indignant, moved away toward the woods, whence all his instincts drew him.

"Let him go," Cam chuckled. "He'll need to chew on many a root an' berry to clean him out before he breaks his winter fast. His nose'll lead him to the right thing; there's naught we can do about it."

"Will he come back, Pa?" Viney cried.

"All that's as may be," Cam said, "but I'd not wonder if we saw a heap more o' the rascal before he finds a mate."

They watched as he moved off up the brush-clad slope, pausing to rummage. He was seeking the waxberry, the natural spring purgative of his kind. It would be three days at least before he ate solid food, Cam said.

That was a strange spring for Bucky, time of change and endings. Time of new beginning too. You could feel it all in the air. The days passed and nothing was done about the place. Cam looked at the truck patch. He took up a handful of earth to see if it was fit to work, knowing well it was, but he made no move to turn it over. He'd made no move to see Doane Shattuck about overdue payments either. Once or twice Bucky'd been on the point of asking why, but refrained. It gave him a queer, floaty feel.

And then one afternoon Doane Shattuck's car was seen coming up the rutty road. It stopped below the clearing and Shattuck came puffing up through the wood lot, heaving his watch-chain belly before him like it was another man. Someone else was sitting in the car. It was Fonse Turner, Bucky saw, Turner who was now Town Marshal as well as Game Warden. Bucky had started down to meet Shattuck with a premonitory bubbling under his breastbone when he saw Cam come out of the woods at the clearing's edge, as if he had been waiting there.

"How d'ye do, how d'ye do, Cam?" Shattuck called

out with a great show of heartiness. "You're looking right well. Heard about your accident in the woods. Glad to see you about again."

"Thank 'e. I'm right as rain again."

Shattuck's sharp eyes were taking in the clearing and the weeds firing up all over the cleared ground. "Looks like you've not turned over anything for planting this spring, Cam."

"Not yet."

"I've been expecting you to drop in and see me for a long time," Shattuck said. "You didn't come, so I came to you."

"Been expectin' you."

"Well, Cam, what's been the trouble? Didn't you recall your time was up in March? I've got our signed agreement right here." He drew a folded paper from his pocket and opened it, his face hunkering down into his three chins.

"I'd not forgotten," Cam said. "I'd not have even if 'twas naught but a handshake agreement."

"Fine, fine! Well, I've come to collect what's owing, Cam, and to wish you well with the place."

He was nice as nice each time he opened his mouth, but Bucky, hovering near, saw the hard, sharp eyes drilling Cam, and the scheme light in their depths. Ma, in some of her puckered moments, had said she wanted him to be a businessman like Doane Shattuck, who lived in the finest house in town and owned a share of the bank and was a "leading citizen." But Bucky felt about Shattuck just as Cam did, who often said: "That feller ain't even a close enemy o' mine," height of scorn in the Swiftwater country.

Cam was saying quietly, "I've some money laid by for you. Two hundred and fifty dollars. The rest I'll have to make up. Figger on goin' to work in the sawmill up at the Forks."

"You owe me nearly twice that, Cam. Four hundred and forty dollars. A bargain's a bargain, both sides, you know. I've kept my end up and I banked on you keeping yours."

Shattuck made out to be mightily peeved and disappointed, but 'twas something very different sliding round now behind his look, Bucky saw. 'Twas pleasure. Yes, Bucky could see the shape of it now.

Cam was unruffled. "I'd a' had it all an' more, but the bottom dropped out o' the fur market this winter. Likely you heard. But I'll make it up at the mill in three-four months—"

"Now, Cam, we signed this agreement in good faith. The same kind of papers I've used with buyers for fifteen years. It says right here you acknowledge the debt in full and in case of failure to pay by the given date you surrender all right and title remaining in said land—"

"No call to read it all out," Cam said. "I know what it says. No call for us to stand here jowerin' either. Talk's a wearyin' vanity, as the poet said. So I'll just say it for you, what you came to tell. My name's wrote there on the paper an' my time's up long gone. I never yet broke given word, signed or swore to. So we'll just be movin' out, quiet an' peaceable. Day after tomorrow we'll be gone from here, so you can call off your bloodhound, Shattuck—" he jerked his head in the direction of Fonse Turner—"an' rest easy. Good day to ye."

Triumph coming that easy broke down Doane Shattuck's face completely. Seemed he didn't dare let it show out in an open, honest way though, good church member that he was. He had to cover it over with words and a show of peeve, as if it were he who was getting the bad end of the bargain. The result left his heavy mouth ropy and writhing in the nest of the fat jowls. Only the eyes remained hard, watching from the fat face like the eyes of Jeth Mellott's old boar hog.

"Now, Calloway," Shattuck sputtered, as if launching a complaint, "I want only what's mine, not a penny more nor less, you know that. I don't aim to be hard."

"Course you don't." Cam was meek as Moses. "You're only livin' up to the law's letter, Shattuck, an' you got a hog-tight agreement there to back you up. Trappin' a man an' skinnin' him is just a part of the land-office game—"

"You've had your chance and a month's grace on top of that. Now the law'll have to take its course." Shattuck pocketed his agreement. His real feelings were coming out now on his face, the mouth still ropy, but with a hard down droop to its looseness. Satisfaction in the porcine eye.

It was Cam's turn for a drilling look. It wasn't the sort Shattuck used. Just a quiet gaze of studious contemplation, behind it a glint of humor. His lean, bronzed, contained face made the other squirm somehow, like an accusation he couldn't answer.

"Well—something else, Calloway?" Shattuck paused on the point of turning away.

"Was just wonderin'," Cam mused, "what 'tis gets into a feller like you when he sees a few dollars in the offing. Did I know that, I'd purely have the answer to the last puzzle in life."

He was still mild as Moses, but Shattuck gave a snort like a bull, and went off down the hill as fast as his town shoes would let him. Bucky approached as Shattuck drove away.

"You heard?" Cam said wearily.

"Yes, Pa."

"I'd a' gone through with it all if Shattuck'd took what we had to offer, but he wouldn't. 'Twas like a sign. Oh,

I been expectin' this for many a day. But Shattuck's within his legal rights. The place is his now."

Bucky said through tight throat: "Doane Shattuck's a scutter!"

"Give him time an' he'll purely beggar himself in beggarin' others," Cam said. "His record'll run before him. 'Fore long there won't be a man in the country'll deal with him. But all that's in the Lord's hands. Now we got to think of movin' again. To me it's no matter, nor you either, I mistrust, Bucky. We've the mind an' the heart an' the body for the deep woods. But your ma'll take it right hard. She's everly contrivin' townward, Lord help her. Oh, there'll be fireworks aplenty."

"What we goin' to do, Pa?" Bucky dropped his head to hide his surge of feeling.

"Move out towards the marsh land, guess we better. It's government land out there. I'll file on it; always wanted to. But now we got to tell all to your ma—about the trimmin' we took on our furs an' the whole sorry mess. One bright thing, we got our fur money now, 'stead o' Shattuck. It'll give us the run o' our teeth till we're squared away in the new place an' that's somethin'. I an' you'll have to pitch in an' build us a new cabin—"

"Shuh, we can put up a better one than this. An' out there's where the geese stop, Pa."

Bucky took this low moment to tell Cam for the first time about Alf Simes' interest in the wild-goose sanctuary and how he'd promised in a way to help. Cam's face actually did light up for a few moments at mention of Alf's name.

"Oh, I've a bonny plan or two to work out in them marshes, son," he said. "Now I want you should go over an' ask for the loan of Jeth Mellott's horse an' wagon for tomorrow, so's we can move our gear. Meanwhiles I'll

130

have it all out with your ma. Figger I'd best do that alone."

Bucky watched as his father moved up toward the house. Cam looked frail somehow, and slack-shouldered.

Bucky's heart was heavy as he took the woods road toward the Mellotts'. But birds were in song all through the woods, the sun and wind were soft, and spring was a yeast in his veins in spite of all. It wouldn't be so bad out there by the marshes. And his long-held plan about the geese could now work out. Of course, Ma'd be fit to take a 'plexy, but she'd get over it in time. At sixteen you couldn't stay sad on such a day, a day so soft and idle and beautiful it fair addled your blood.

Soon he was whistling as he walked along.

PART THREE

18

Now the woods had closed in on the Calloways for fair. Their new cabin going up at the edge of the marsh land was five miles from Swiftwater, so that the townfolk saw even less of them these days. But the town laughed and had its say about it all. Old fiddle-footed "Never-Stay-Put" had moved on again, lost all but his shirt this time, 'twas said, way he had so many times before. A general snort was heard when it was learned what land Cam had filed on.

"Why, that marsh land's pretty much nothing even as a timber claim."

It was a stiff spring for the Calloways on more than one count, living in a crude bark shelter while their cabin was raised, cooking over campfires.

"Mis' Calloway an' that gal young'un of hers out there too, fancy that!" the gossip went round.

As if it wasn't strife enough just to live, there was strife now between Cam and his wife, cropping out in harsh arguments and bitter accusing silences, in wrangling over the smallest things. Cam had chosen well the place for the new cabin and was starting to clear away when Ma came out of the lean-to stormy mad, having picked out an entirely different spot the night before. A house was summat of a woman's concern, at least she hoped so, Ma proclaimed, her eyes glinting dangerously at her man, and she marked out just where she wanted it built, and how. There was more than one reason why it would be best to build it where Cam had chosen, but he gave in.

It was that way with all that came up. Bucky could see a measure of right on both sides and he was torn between the two, miserable that dispute should darken the brightness of these days of exciting new venture. But as time went on his condonation passed to Cam. Ma had gone wilful-blind. She flared up like a priming pan at any who contraried her.

"We drove our ducks to a bad market, comin' to this buried place," she'd said at the outset and let the stigma lay.

Once Bucky had seen her crying, holding her fisher cape in her lap. Only once had she worn it in to town in all the winter months. He pitied her. He pitied them both. Ma had practically given over talk and her prolonged silence was like a condemnation. It lay upon Cam like a blight, dulling hope and heart for new things. Bucky worried. It was times like this that filled Cam with his restless migratory urge.

There was a deadening near their cabin site, and here Cam and Bucky set to cutting logs. They chose only sapless, seasoned trees that would not warp, darkened to gold-brown by the weather and showing the intricate patterns the bark worms had made on their smooth surfaces. It was heavy work felling them and harder still moving the felled logs to their clearing, with the aid of skids and a rough, weather-gray stone-boat. Less patient men would have given it up as hopeless.

On the third morning, as they labored with sweat in their eyes, their sight gone blurry, a wagon came rolling out from the edge of the trees.

"Mornin', Cam—mornin', Bucky." It was big Jeth Mellott who sat on the wagon seat. Jeth flung the reins to the ground and the two men dropped overside.

"Foundation most laid, I see," Jeth yelled in his foghorn voice, which always sounded as if he were hailing a neighbor in the next forty. "Thought ye might like the loan of the team, Cam, for a day or two."

Cam was nigh dumbfounded with gratitude and couldn't word his thanks, for he'd had no idea how they were to haul in and hoist the great ridge log alone, nor the longer logs that were to run the length of the cabin.

Before Jeth's team was hitched to the first log another wagon came creaking up—Luke Callant's, Luke on the seat, with young Will Nagle beside him and Mrs. Callant on the back seat holding a big basket. Word of the Calloways' house raising had sped round like a fire in dry grass, it seemed, though it had been neither Cam nor Bucky who spread it. 'Twas all Jeth Mellott's doing, Bucky guessed.

"Oh, there's nothin' like a good log rollin' for gatherin' folk together," Jeth roared. "Look at that. There's big Luke and his woman. Been touchy with me as a mule in fly time for a year past, Luke has, ever since I shot a buck he'd been trailin'. But he'll be jokin' and pawin' my shoulder 'fore noon. Light, hitch, an' come right in," he bellowed to the approaching wagon.

Soon there was the ring of six axes instead of two, interspersed with the thunderous crash of falling trees. Before the third tree was down little Ira Eddy had bobbed out of the thickets carrying another ax. Hard behind him came Wiley Meeks. All of them Cam's special friends. Bucky's heart swelled.

By midday it was a real old-time log rolling. Three teams were snaking in the big logs. Four big flat boulders had been dragged in, one for each corner of the house, to make all doubly solid. Cam, wielding an adze, had no sooner finished flattening the sides of a new cut log than it was seized and notched and heaved into place in the rising wall by half a dozen waiting hands. A cross-cut saw growled and snarled, cutting out the logs where the doors and windows were to be. Old Sounder went lolloping like a daft one from group to group of workers, and old Scissorbill, in his cage on a pine bough, went hoarse from hawing.

Baskets of food, enough to feed a logging crew, had been brought along in the wagons and with Mrs. Callant to talk to and help lay it out, Ma was drawn out of her sulling. She even came out with some new ideas for altering the cabin a mite. With just a few changes, she said, half the cabin could be two-storied, so that Bucky could sleep up under the eaves as he'd always liked. And two small windows should be cut at once, just above where the stove would be, so she could see what was toward as she cooked.

"Yes, you'd best make your stand flat-footed if you're to get what you want," Mrs. Callant told her, "before the men build it past all changing."

Cam, delighted at any show of interest after Ma's siege of silence, carried out the new ideas at once. Two smooth peeled uprights supporting a notched cross-log soon marked off the half loft and an hour later it was already ceiled with straight young pine poles.

At the midday feast round the campfire there were jokes and all manner of tall-tale telling.

"Step up to once, you boys. I'll wait. The old come first, you know," yelled Jeth Mellott.

"Pshaw! Looks before age! Wiley, you lead out."

"Since you ain't got 'em, you need an extry bait o' food, Ira. Haw, haw, haw."

Ma brought forth part of a leg of venison and some of her famous biscuits and wild-gooseberry jam. The men ate till it seemed a wonder they could tote their vittles. Big Luke Callant, sinking away his third plateful of deermeat, exclaimed:

"Grandpa's toenail sure slipped an' tore the sheet again, Mis' Calloway! Like I always say, you got 'em all stopped fer cookin'—up an' down the river—money, marbles, or chalk!"

Ma made as if it were nothing, smoothing down her dress in front, the way she did when she was pleased, but she was a different woman the rest of the day.

This was a time when the men would have relished a bottle of something, but there was not a sniff of liquor here, nor even mention of it, in quiet deference to Cam, whose weakness was known to all. Bucky was detailed to help Ma and Mrs. Callant pass things about and press food and coffee on all. Almighty polite and unnatural he was about it, the way Ma got when townfolk happened to call.

By the time owllight came there were chips and sawdust a foot deep and the new house was good as built. A better, bigger house than the one they'd moved out of, too. It all went to show what could be done when eight good axmen set their minds on a thing. All the biggest logs were well in place, even the ridgepole and rafters were laid, and there was scarce any heavy work left, just the roofing and clay chinking and doweling out the door and window frames with frow and auger. 'Twas a downright miracle that had happened since morning and none of the Calloways could find words to speak of it.

Cam stood beside Ma saying thank you to the company as they made ready to leave, exactly as such things had been done back in pioneer days, both of them smiling at everyone and each other.

"Bosh an' moonshine! 'Twant nothing," Jeth Mellott bellowed. "Why, we'd all ought to thank you folks for givin' us such a get-together."

"That's a fact, Cam. Not even a good marryin' or a buryin' could a' touched this. Ain't had me such a time since the hogs et my brother-in-law," whickered Wiley Meeks. He gave Cam a whack on the back, whooping louder than any at his own joke.

A half moon was sailing up above the pinetops like a yellow boat before the workers, with much shouting and joshing back and forth, piled into the three wagons and filed away down the winding woods road. Bucky stood looking after them; a flush burned in his cheeks. It seemed to have gone to his head a bit, the unexpected friendliness of all these folk in the face of the town's long-held disparagement.

Suddenly he ran forward to the edge of the clearing and called:

"We ain't no ways thanked you yet for all you done, but we're like to find a way, come fur season. Just you wait!"

His voice rang through the woods. An echo replied, dwindling, hollow, far off among the hackmatacks. A hail from the wagons told they'd heard.

He turned back abashed, avoiding the firelight, and vaguely heard Cam's voice:

"You done right, son, you spoke from the heart."

He walked on into the darkness of the wood where the 'poor-wills called, heading for the lake. He'd never been in such a blissful pother; he felt he'd never sleep again, for this had been an epic day in the Calloway family history. 'Twas only what all days ought to be like, though, Bucky thought. Oh, did there anywhere exist the immense event, the great surprise of a single day that could wholly satisfy his young, vital impatience? He walked on and on through the fragrant dark, watching the dance of fireflies in the woods, humming weird tunes into the breeze.

An hour later he found himself rounding home through the townward end of Cam's old timber claim, following a winding wood road. He halted presently with an actual start at a turn in the road. Ahead of him was a great gap in the woods where no gap had been before, wide and white and spectral-looking in the pale wash of moonlight. It was a fresh cutting of hundreds of prime trees. Trimmed logs lay piled and ready for hauling beside the road, a big truck-trailer standing there too with a sign on it: SHATTUCK & TURNER LUMBER COMPANY. So that was the cute of Shattuck's play that day at the cabin while Fonse Turner waited in the car. Already the two were fattening off the land Cam had lost.

PROPERTY OF
FRANKFORT SCHUYLER CENTRAL
HIGH SCHOOL LIBRARY
FRANKFORT, NEW YORK 13340

19

IN EARLY MAY CAM AND BUCKY PUT IN A SMALL TRUCK
patch behind the new cabin. But always Cam went
too deep in the woods for crops to thrive. Father and
son further showed addle-pated, so far as the town
went, by planting a straggling field of corn down toward the marsh land, of all places. They didn't plant in
orderly hills, but in stringy rows; they didn't plow deep
either, merely roughed up the seed beds of grass and
weed with the shovel. Swiftwater had its idea about
corn.

"Why, that marsh propity wouldn't bring five bushel
to the acre!"

The spring had been rainy. The boggy edges of the
new cornfield stayed soaked all month. Weeds fired up
in places ahead of the corn. That stretched another
smile over the countryside. The whole place looked
frowsy—patches where the corn had the upper hand,
spots where it seemed a plain toss-up. Townfolk
couldn't let the matter rest. They drove out Sundays
and had their say.

"Aye cod, nobody but Cam Calloway'd be guilty of a cornfield like that."

But Cam and Bucky kept their own counsel.

It was in May, too, that Bridie Mellott came down with scarlet fever. The Calloways were slow in hearing. Bucky thought little about it at first. Then he heard Ma talk about it. Purely worried about Bridie, she seemed. Oh, she knew a sight about diseases, Ma did; she recounted tales of yellow jack, malaria, the bloody flux, and only God knew what that she'd seen in her youth. She'd known many a young thing cut off before prime by this same scarlet plague, she said.

One day she made up some bread risin' and sent it along with some sourdough and boneset herb to the Mellotts by Bucky. He was to ask if there was ought to be done to help.

Bucky found a big red sign tacked up on the Mellott porch to warn folk away. Jeth answered his knock, but couldn't ask him in; the house was quarantined. Bridie was sicker than anyone he'd ever seen before or since, Jeth said. Bucky went on to town thinking about the quarantine, thinking about Bridie looking scarlet. It could be Bridie was going to die, he thought, and all his being rose up to ward off this besetting evil.

For six weeks the red sign hung on the Mellotts' porch. At long last it was taken down and Bucky least of all was prepared for what came then. A slim, overgrown girl with freckles had gone into her house at the end of April, stayed with scarlet fever for six weeks, and emerged—"the prettiest girl in the whole durn country."

Big Luke Callant had said that, and Bucky found it true. She had come out like the juneberry, that is only a slim pile wand one day and the next is all blossoms, and lovelier than anything else in the woods. The freckles that had dotted Bridie's cheeks like a dusting of nutmeg were gone; her skin had turned clear and pale as the white tulip laurel. Seemed you could see right down into it an inch or more—the kind of skin that went with flaming sorrel hair. That hair had deepened till it glowed like the bonfires of fall. Her eyes were blue as wild asters against the whiteness of her skin.

Bucky met her on the road to town on a day in early June. She wore a fluffy summer dress. He wanted to stop and talk, or maybe walk a piece with her. Words formed, but he couldn't let them out. He just mumbled "H'lo," and strode past with quickening pace, as if something almighty important were driving him. The bright quick look she gave him and the tilt of her gleaming head as she passed transfixed him with joy. Pretty as a spotted fawn, she was; her eyes, deep and wide and soft, under the mist of her hair, seemed to scoop something out of the pit of his chest, and take it with them off to some secret, lovely place she knew, leaving him hollowed out and pining.

The picture of her remained with him all day, the memory of his own goose foolishness reddening his face and causing the sweat to pop out. Whatever had come over him? 'Twas her downright loveliness. Prettier than anything he'd ever seen, she was; he had to admit. It riled him someway, but there it was. He'd strode off sore as a baited badger, but mad with growing love. Love that didn't know itself, but took it out in irritation. Oh, he'd wanted to talk with her more than anything else, but couldn't bring himself to it. Months alone had left him woods-shy and tongue-halted.

He saw her numerous times in the weeks that followed. Passing the Mellott place was a regular thing

141

now, though 'twas well out of his way. She seemed to like making folk come to her. Other eyes pulled her, too: Whit Turner's. Bucky saw her once with Whit in Mc-Kay's drugstore, the two of them having colored drinks in tall glasses, laughing together. Whit had developed a hard bright smile and an assurance that rushed out of every feature and expressed itself in every gesture. Pleasing enough it seemed to Bridie. Bucky went off home in a dull fury.

That afternoon he studied himself in Ma's square of mirror for the first time in months. A mite of repair work needed here and there. The fuzz on cheek and chin was no longer down; he'd gone a bit too deep in the woods for any woman's taste. He bided his time and next morning, when the house was clear, he got out Cam's razor. Before he knew it there was a cut on his chin. Nothing much though. He'd heard other boys in town fingering a cut and saying casual-like: "My razor slipped this morning." He tried to slick down his dark mop of hair, but it sadly needed cutting.

Later he squirmed when he found Cam eying him in quiet contemplation and with a touch of amusement.

"Looks like Bucky's a man growed now, for sure," Cam remarked at large. "'Fore we know it he'll be fixin' to marry an' leave us. Got the girl picked out, son?"

Bucky said sullenly he had no time for girls.

"My sakes," Ma said, looking round. "Time enough to go soft over girls when he's twenty-one or there-abouts."

Bucky went her one better and said that *never* would be better still. He got up abruptly and left the house.

All the same he went on seeing Bridie in his mind. She nestled there sweet as honey in a comb. Oh, she could have ridden him a-bug-hunting to the cliff and made him jump over and think it fun, if she'd a mind. He caught himself making pictures of her being with him in the woods as she used to be, day-long tramps together, two tin plates for their eating, things a lot different. Always with these thoughts came the lonely-happy feel he had only in the woods with Cam. It was that way with all the deepest things to Bucky; with the thought of something sweet and happy a lonesome something came hard on its heels. And no wonder. He could never again come near such wonder as Bridie had now. Pretty rough he'd been with her a year back when she'd wanted to follow him around. He'd purely fixed it for himself. Now she'd no mind for the woods or him. She'd turned to things and comforts and town ways—like Ma.

Such a fool he was these days, thin and rabbity, all run to arms and legs and stumbling feet. When he went in to town he felt his isolation as never before, felt himself actually being walled off, driven out. Sometimes a black brew surged up in him, a ruining hatred, but he had Cam's detachment to fall back on.

From the dooryard he could see the scorn and sneers on the faces of team drivers going by, looking at the cornfield. No fences up. Those few who cared to could cross the Calloway land quite as if it had been deserted as aforetime. Hard to stand, keeping quiet about it all, pretending they were serious in their farming. It was such a gamble he and Cam were making.

Twice during those spring months Bucky went to Alf Simes' house to talk more about the geese. Each time he'd been at a low and hopeless ebb and each time he'd come away all fired anew with hope and reinforced with zeal, his mind and being scourged and sandblasted by the fiery flow of Alf's rhetoric, in the face of which all undertakings seemed not only possible but already won. The geese hadn't stopped that spring, but what of that? They'd stop for Cam's corn in the fall, Alf said. Already he was getting in his work on Bucky's plan. 'Twouldn't be long before the town would be seeing the light of his reason, never fear.

20

KEG, THE CALLOWAYS' TAME BEAR, HAD NOT BEEN DO-
ing so well. For a week after he had unholed from the
root cellar, he had wandered disconsolately through the
deserted March woods, lean and cold and brittle of fur,
and nauseated by the spring sickness of his kind. Instinct
had told him what to do about that and in time his ill-
ness passed away under a purge of waxberries and soap-
berries that grew in abundance on their ground-creep-
ing vines. After that he felt better than ever before in
his life, stronger, wilder, happier—and hungrier.

Prompted by that evanescent sixth sense which flick-
ers on in the wiser among us, he was led to several rotting logs which were full of grubs, and he spent some
blissful hours ripping the wood to pieces and savoring
the new, rich feeding that was dear to every ursine
palate. But he craved something else terribly. Stronger
feeding, and companionship. The spell of the wintry
woods still lay heavy over all things; the stillness increased, not broken by the hundred and one crepitant
little sounds of the thaw. Not another bear was stirring

in all the woods. There were rabbits and squirrels, however, and great horned owls, but they were no good to Keg, logy and slow-muscled as he was.

The call of the wild wrought vaguely upon him. He wandered by day and by night, knowing that he must see behind the ranges. He made out to hunt as he went, but a thankless business it was in a frogless, fishless, honeyless world, a world where no pans of scraps were ever set out for a fellow. He had not forgotten the Calloways and one day he made for the Calloway clearing straight as the crow flies. There he found nothing but silence and desertion and experienced the first great shock of his life.

His trepidation gave way to an almost human sense of grief as the afternoon wore on with no sign of his friends' return. That night he slept, intermittently, close by the kitchen door, rising at times to move disconsolately about the cabin, expecting constantly that the door might open and his friends magically reappear and call him. But nothing of the sort occurred, even when rain set in toward morning and drove him to the shed.

With the morning light his hopes were rekindled. Until noon he roamed about searching for scraps of food, rummaging through the rubbish pile. He had had about enough of the bootless game of stalking the thickets, but by afternoon, when his appetite had grown to an incubus that would not let him rest, he departed once more into the woods.

Two mornings later he came again to the Calloway clearing. He scratched at each door in turn; then, in a passion of appeal calculated to melt the hearts of his unfeeling friends, he rose on his hind legs and paraded back and forth before the door, doing his tricks. But house and clearing remained callously deserted, as before.

For the next two weeks this state of affairs continued. Keg would linger close to the cabin until gnawing hunger literally drove him into the woods, but always he would return. By the end of a month his expectancy had dulled, but clearing and cabin continued to be magnetic. Something was lacking in the deep woods and it was the Calloways he yearned for. And not all the frogs in the ponds or the squirrels in the trees could alleviate the lack of human companionship, or ever would again, it seemed.

It was about this time that the cabin's draw was doubly increased for him by the fact that he gained access to the interior. A windstorm had blown open the rear door. Keg joyfully shifted his quarters from the clearing to the cabin kitchen. It was good to be in the old familiar quarters. The rusted cookstove was still there and there were many gratifying scents of the recent occupants. Ensconced within the log walls Keg felt somehow closer to the culmination of his quest.

The wonderful golden weeks of May and June drifted by, and an abundance of berries began to be evident along the open hillsides. Keg needed no initiation to recognize these immemorial standbys of his clan. His wanderings now took him in ever-widening circles away from the clearing, but the richest feeding failed to satisfy his vague unrest.

It was at the end of June, as he was making a return journey to the cabin, that Keg experienced a delightful surprise. As he was rooting in a glade a man stepped out of the thickets. It was Bucky Calloway, out squirreling with Cam's rifle. Keg did not recognize him at once. Bucky called out laughingly and at the sound Keg's heart gave a joyful surge. With a glad bawl he shuffled forward and immediately his nose apprised him that this was Bucky Calloway, with whom he had romped and wrestled, reappearing magically from the place in which he had been hiding so long. Keg rose up on his hind legs and fell upon the boy with an unrestrained delight that carried with it the threat of mayhem.

Time and again Bucky had wondered what had become of the half-grown cub. He'd have liked to accommodate Keg now with the loving wrestle for which his old pet yearned, but Keg's growth had been as phenomenal in the past few months as his own. For safety of life and limb he had to beat off the four-hundred-pound bear with sharp cuffs and peremptory cries, for Keg was quite unaware of his own strength and weight.

When his joy had somewhat subsided Keg fell to nosing into all Bucky's pockets as of old. There were no lumps of sugar, but Bucky had part of his lunch left, which Keg bolted with satisfaction. Bucky sat watching with a glow of pride and pleasure, eager now to lead Keg home and hear what Cam would say, for his father had never thought to see the cub again.

He rose presently and moved away in the woods, Keg following some distance behind, but stopping often to nose into holes and crannies. After half a mile or so he fell far behind and Bucky went on alone. But Keg's nose was none too good in the puzzling out of trails and in his brain there was but one spot associated with Bucky Calloway—the old deserted cabin. Thither he returned at nightfall by roundabout ways, only to find the place empty as before. Once more the Calloways had somehow eluded him. Amazed and sorrowful, he prowled about the cabin. It was all a terrible mistake, he felt sure; one of those senseless, thoughtless slips to which humans seemed prone. Now he was back again in the same forlorn state he'd been in the night before.

Bucky had run the last half mile home that afternoon, full of the news of his meeting with Keg, only to find that Cam was away. Ma threw up her hands with a gesture of resignation when she heard.

"Sakes alive, Bucky, don't tell me you've lured that lollopin' bruiser back here to eat off us for the summer!" she cried. "He ain't only another mouth to feed, he'd be five or six mouths now, an' prob'ly there's nothing viciouser in the woods."

"Huh, not hardly," Bucky laughed. "He ain't changed a mite. Rared up and like to have kissed me, he was that glad to see me. He was noseyin' along behind me, headed this way when I left him."

"I purely hope somethin' lay-ways him before he gets here," Ma said. "Nobody in this house ever thinks of cost but me. For the first time in two years we've had our chance to get ahead a mite, with that bear an' his appetite away in the woods."

"Aw, Ma. There's plenty berries and mast in the woods now. I promise he won't eat off us. I'll get him honey and fish to eat. Lordy, but I've missed seeing him around."

Little Viney, who had just come in, set up a wail of pleasure and anticipation when she heard. Ever since Keg had left in the spring she'd been pining for him. For nearly two years Keg had taken the place of all the play-pretties, dolls, and oddmedods she hadn't had in her lonely backwoods childhood.

"I'm going out and find Keg now," she announced. "Whereabouts was it you saw him, Bucky?"

Because of Keg's bulk and strength Bucky went with her for safety's sake. They followed Bucky's back trail for nearly a mile, but saw nothing of Keg. By the time owllight came the bear had still not appeared. Ma breathed a sigh of relief.

"Looks like nature'd takened a hand in our favor this once," she said, but Viney cried herself to sleep that night.

The next few days she took to woods roaming in the hope of finding her pet again. One still afternoon about a week later, she had wandered far from the home clearing along the bank of a little stream. Timber-raised and used to lonely playing, she'd entered into that magic realm that gregarious children never know and grownups wouldn't have credited even if she could have told them of it, grownups managing to forget all such things with maturity. For two hours she'd wandered here, there, and everywhere, playing in her own way, vying with the red squirrels in search of nuts, with the willow wrens in the seeking out of secret places, and with the big paint-green frogs in plumbing the depths of the woodland pools. She'd heard scents and colors, seen sounds, and smelled joys in the summer air, all at one and the same time, in the instinctive way that young birds and animals do.

Once she'd crawled into a hollow tree and heard a weird, boogerish sound far above, and looking up she'd seen two phosphorescent eyes glaring at her far up in the hollow black bole. But 'twas only a horned owl. Later, creeping through a spruce grove, she'd looked up and seen a big, gray, tuft-eared bobcat lying out along a limb not fifty feet away and she'd had no fear of it at all.

About mid-afternoon she'd come to the banks of a little stream. Now she was making boats out of rolled bark and sending boatloads of frightened folk down the rushing stream to the far-off sea, or so she hoped. Her people were pine cones and acorns and she sang to them with each launching.

Presently a disturbing sensation that she was not alone

began to steal over the child—a sense that unfriendly eyes were close by. She hardly credited it at first, but it persisted. Finally she stood up and strove to penetrate the blue-black shadows.

Then her heart gave a violent surge and she wished mightily she had taken heed of those semiconscious warnings earlier. Something subtle as a shifting cloud had caused her to glance upward and there, framed in a tangle of windfall, she saw a round, malign head with two ocher-green eyes that fixed her with cruel intensity. It was old Fire Eyes himself.

He'd been there a long time, had Fire Eyes, watching Viney Calloway at play. Oh, this was not the first time he had followed the girl in her woods wandering. More than a year back he had taken to watching her in her own clearing, knowing well that he could obliterate her with a single pounce. But mighty killer that he was, he had never yet taken human life. Each time he had shadowed her, the one part frenzied daring had come a bit closer to prevailing over the nine parts sheer cowardice that composed his nature, but an instinctive awe of man continued to hold him from success.

Today, in this lonely spot, he had lashed himself to the point of lethal action. And like the fiery heart of the hawk, the blood lust of Fire Eyes, fully roused, was not to be turned aside. Imagination had wrought upon him till lurid flames burned in his gooseberry eyes and he could fairly smell and savor the tender flesh of his prospective prey.

Abruptly the panther's head withdrew for an instant, to reappear at another spot several feet closer. There was a suggestion of the long tawny body now, the color of gunmetal, a shaft of cold fear in the purpose to be felt in its sinister movements.

Breaking the spell of the dreadful watching eyes, Viney turned and fled along the stream bank. A glance flung to the rear showed the panther gliding serpentwise through the thickets, coming on.

21

$\mathcal{E}$MBOLDENED BY THE SIGHT OF THE CHILD RUNNING
away, Fire Eyes covered the ground in long, undulating
bounds, keeping to the undergrowth. Viney ran now
with frank abandon and with all the strength she had.
She had never before known fear of wild things, but she
was terrified now and whimpered as she ran, fearing
each moment to be struck down. But her woods sense
did not leave her; she knew just where she was—less
than half a mile from the old deserted Calloway cabin
—and toward it, in spite of panic, she turned in her
flight, knowing there would be refuge there.

Old Fire Eyes was fascinated by the ancient game of
chasing a desperate quarry. He came on, always keeping
to cover, never getting closer, yet never falling behind.
The natural indirection of all cats was all that delayed
the fatal issue in those first vital minutes.

Keg, as it happened, was rummaging disconsolately
about the deserted Calloway clearing. Rounding a corner of the house in late afternoon, he raised his head
eagerly at sound of a human cry that came floating to
him from somewhere out at the edge of the woods.

153

He paused to peer with his myopic little eyes and saw a girl come dashing into the clearing, calling out desperately as she ran. Then he saw that it was Viney. He lumbered joyously forward.

The child in her panic flight had reached the clearing back of the cabin in the very nick of time. Fire Eyes was gliding along in the rear, but the instinct for keeping to cover kept him busy utilizing every possible clump of undergrowth in his path.

Her breath coming in a sobbing double action, the child spurted across the wood lot with the last of her strength, the panther now but a couple of rods behind. The rear cabin door stood mercifully open. 'Twas then, when she was only halfway across the clearing, that there came a fresh shaft of terror at the apparition of Keg's lumbering form as he rounded the cabin and made straight for the youngster, mouth open. She plunged in at the open door, just as old Fire Eyes, literally beside himself with fury and blood-madness, came lancing through the air to land upon the neck and shoulders of the bear.

Toward the middle of that afternoon, Bucky, rounding home after a desultory hunt, had come upon the broad, rounded tracks of Fire Eyes in the damp earth on the bank of a little stream. He knew that trail by its exceptional size. And as he had done a score of times before, he turned aside to follow it, for the tracks showed to be less than an hour old. For a thousand yards along the bank he worked out the trail, noting where Fire Eyes had crouched belly-down for intervals to watch and wait. What had the old killer been stalking, he wondered.

He was a long time puzzling out the tracks where they finally left the stream bank and when he did he was startled to find mingled with them the footprints of a child. It could be that Fire Eyes had grown bold

154

enough to stalk human prey for a change, if that prey happened to be a little tyke like Viney. Long since Bucky's eye had taken note of a circling buzzard whose slow gyres of flight were dropping lower and lower above the forest.

Bucky hurried forward now, his quick eye reading sign as he went. He came upon deepened toe marks and saw that the child was in full flight. His heart began to pound, for Fire Eyes' trail too had become a series of long bounds, each deep paw mark scored round by prints of unsheathed claws. Bucky was running too, soundless in his felt-soled shoes.

Stumbling through thickets, he sped toward the deserted cabin by the shortest possible route, pausing to shout now and then through cupped hands. He arrived panting at the edge of the old clearing just in time to witness the tableau of old Fire Eyes locked in fiendish battle with a black bear—a bear which even in the thresh of conflict Bucky recognized as Keg.

Ordinarily bear and panther tacitly avoid one another in their comings and goings, through mutual and well-warranted respect of prowess, each being something of a forest king in his own right. But in this instance all such inhibitions had been swept aside. When Keg suddenly appeared round the corner of the cabin, it seemed to old Fire Eyes a direct attempt to rob him of the prey he had so patiently stalked—the most unforgivable crime in the wild. Instantly he had sprung forward to annihilate this hereditary foe, for the feud between bear and panther is age-old.

Keg had been flung forward on his nose as the two hundred pounds of death, armed with four sets of saber claws, landed on his back. Immediately the slow, deadly wrath of his phlegmatic nature was lashed to flame. In his nostrils was the alien scent of his attacker. Rearing upward with a bawl of rage, he flung all his great strength into the struggle, mouth open in the savage caricature of a grin that is the fighting mask of the black bear.

The vantage at the outset was all with the panther. He rode his adversary like some giant leech, with talons that clung like grappling hooks and ripped like razors, and he was busy every second.

Though it was his first real battle, Keg knew he was being killed. The tactics of Fire Eyes were swift, bloody, and horrible, for endurance was not in his arsenal. He must kill quickly, before his enemy's superior strength and weight could be brought into play. His back bent to an arch of whalebone, he raked madly, at the same time cutting in with his long fangs toward the life arteries in Keg's thick, furry neck. . . . Death screaming and fetid-breathed, tearing at his windpipe; death gouging at his eyes.

Staggering under the killer's weight, Keg battled silently now to gain some hold. The devastation wrought was appalling. Blood smeared his chest. He brought up against the log wall of the cabin and instinct prompted him to batter himself against it and scrape his opponent off. But all his efforts failed to dislodge his deathly rider.

He flung himself on his side. One of the panther's paws came in reach, and Keg's jaws closed upon it and locked. The cat creature emitted a scream—the inability of all felines to endure pain. The murderous clamp on Keg's throat slackened, and in a moment he had heaved himself over and grappled the bulk of the enemy on an equal footing. All his great strength was brought into play in a wrestler's grip that strained the panther's ribs to cracking, but never for an instant did his grip on Fire Eyes' leg relax. An old feud was being settled now, for good and all. Mighty hunter that he was, Fire Eyes had tackled at last someone who was his match.

The panther's first mad fury turned into something like insanity. The tawny beast's struggles showed no reason now, while Keg, though desperately wounded, fought grimly on.

Through the cabin window Bucky had seen Viney's frightened face and he knew that she was safe. Closer and closer he moved across the clearing, his nearness unsensed by either beast. His rifle was ready to exact the final penalty from old Fire Eyes the moment opportunity presented. But in the surge of the conflict he dared not fire for fear of killing Keg. He found himself shouting encouragement to his old pet.

It seemed an eternity to Bucky before Fire Eyes' long, lean body seemed to give way. There came a fiendish squawl, then the sounds of conflict diminished, until there were only a few low snarlings to be heard and the ruckle of worrying jaws. Keg had torn his opponent loose and brought one great forearm down on his spine like a pile driver. A second time the paw descended. A few more snakelike flounders and the spark of the panther's life snuffed out.

It was a minute or so before Keg realized his victory. As if to complete his vengeance, he continued to beat and rend the inert heap of flesh with teeth and claws till it resembled nothing that had ever walked. His fury finally appeased, he fell to doctoring his wounds. Then, seeing Bucky Calloway standing near, he abruptly rose and ambled toward him in sudden, lolloping friendliness.

Out from the cabin dashed Viney, rushing into Bucky's arms as to a haven. She'd have run straight into the arms of Keg, too, to tug lovingly at his hairy chest, but Bucky held her back.

"Best let him be, Viney," he warned. "He's just found

out he's a big one an' a wild one, the wildest, wooliest thing on four legs an' the almightiest fighter these woods have ever seen. He's a whoppin' big bruiser now, an' he's apt to forget himself an' crack a few more ribs in play without knowin' it."

Bucky had some of his lunch left and this he laid out for Keg. Meantime Viney told and retold the hair-raising events of an afternoon in the woods, and by degrees he was able to piece together the story.

It became evident that Keg's wounds hurt grievously. After whimpering and laving them with soothing tongue for a time, he turned and shuffled away into the forest, where instinct would lead him to the best woods healing for his kind. Bucky stood watching till the shadows swallowed him up. With him went Bucky's benediction and a host of memories, the flavor and the poignancy of countless days of boyhood that would never return, as Keg quite possibly would never return. For he was a grown bear now and by another year he'd likely have no further interest in humans or their ways.

Bucky got out his knife then and knelt beside the sorry remains of old Fire Eyes. There was little left to skin out of that infamous killer, but the legs and the oversize feet remained intact. Every scrap of that tattered hide Bucky meant to preserve, to back up the tale, which would surely be told and retold down the years, of how the Calloways' tame bear had met and killed the famous Swiftwater panther and saved a child's life.

PROPERTY OF
FRANKFORT SCHUYLER CENTRAL
HIGH SCHOOL LIBRARY
FRANKFORT, NEW YORK 13340

22 ~~~~~~~~~~~~

*I*T WAS ON THE FIRST OF JULY THAT MR. DELL FRASER, the hardware salesman, came again to Swiftwater on his semiannual visit. He arrived from the city at four o'clock one hot afternoon and did Stemline's and the hardware store before closing time at six, a boresome and tedious business.

"Not a stone turned since I was here last. This town needs me; she's paralyzed," Mr. Fraser thought, walking down the main street.

Supper at the Lakeview Hotel, Swiftwater's only hostelry, and he the only transient guest. The name itself bored him. "There are seven hundred and fifty 'Lakeview' hotels and boardinghouses through this neck of the woods, and not the buzz of a new idea in any one of 'em."

As he relaxed on the veranda, the last of the sunset glinting on the distant stretch of lake, Hayes, the hotel man, and others sat around or lingered in passing.

"You call this hot?" Dell Fraser inquired. "Why this is sitting out in the cool dew. Down in the city they're taking their sheets out to the fire escapes tonight and

159

in many a town only fifty-sixty miles away. Why don't you let the big towns know what you've got here?"

"Yes, guess it must have been pretty hot down in the city today," said Hamey, the undertaker.

"Why don't you let 'em know what you've got?" Mr. Fraser demanded again. "Somebody's going to wake up this town. Somebody's going to pull the city people out to these cool beaches. What you need first is a key line!"

"A what?" said Hayes.

"A key line to designate your town—a line to make 'em talk, make 'em come. You've got to have a key line to a town, a car, or a business nowadays. The right one's worth a million."

Pondering ensued, but no enthusiasm. Mr. Fraser seemed irritated. Presently a brisk rapping was heard on the walk, and a lean old man, cane in hand, came stumping round the corner. The loungers perked up noticeably. Greetings were hearty, and Mr. Fraser heard the name Alf Simes. A place was made for the newcomer beside the city man.

Old Alf often held forth on the Lakeview's veranda, times when his own porch failed to draw a crowd. Many a townsman was chary of the old man, not a few were outright enemies, and wished him ill, yet these things were forgotten when they came in radius of Alf's voice. They were swept and held by the magic of it, played with and mesmerized as though a searching wind blew among them.

Alf took over tonight as usual, in spite of the city guest. Mr. Fraser listened with tolerant humor at first, tabbing Alf as a laughable backwoods character. But within ten minutes he was spellbound without realizing it, relaxing, sighing at times, chuckling, guffawing loudly as his idling mind and flaccid nerves were filled or taken hold of by the deft play of that silver tongue. Before a half hour was up, however, Mr. Fraser was convinced that he was a power to be reckoned with.

Alf had made a recent trip to the city and he retailed his adventures there. He had been whizzed round the city in high-powered cars. He'd gone down into the bowels of a submarine that lay in the harbor, he'd paid a dollar for a single shot of second-rate hooch, and he'd seen women dancing in a honky-tonk arrayed in nothing but three inches of silk. He'd gotten into such a city-hurry to get nowhere that he'd been going up in the clouds in an airplane when his son Hance had come onto him and stopped him.

In a lull Hamey the undertaker asked Alf to name the most outstanding achievement of this puerile and decadent age, daring him to point out the milestone that marked the furthest limit of human foolishness and stupidity. Alf answered without hesitation that the automobile and the bombing plane were pegged about equal for the honor and way out in front of everything that had been thought of since Bryan's free silver.

Presently Alf veered round to his fox farm. He'd started out with a single pair of black fox and by midwinter he figured to see his investment pay off in prime fur at a rate of some six hundred per cent. Market fur of the future was going to be farm-raised, not trapped, Alf claimed. It was plain as the neck on an ostrich.

"Yes," said Dell Fraser, "there'll be fox farms and mink and sable and otter farms. It's all part of progress."

"You mighty come a-right it is," Alf said.

Presently Mr. Fraser was led to inquire: "Say, whatever became of that kid who fought over the wild goose last fall?"

"Oh, Bucky Calloway. Why, he was in town just a while ago. Up and slipped away the way he always does," Hayes said. "He won't be with us much longer—"

"What do you mean—bad lungs?"

"Bucky's lungs are all right, only he'll be going the way of his father, one of these days."

"Oh I recall. His father was what you might call itinerary," chuckled Mr. Fraser. He became reminiscent. "I keep thinking of that kid and that night, seeing the geese go over and hearing them talk from the lake in the room upstairs—kind of tonic about it, and I'll bet there's fifty thousand men and boys just like me down in the city. Just say 'wild goose' to 'em and they'd come to life. You fellows don't know what you've got here. These beaches are going to be worth millions! One key line about geese and Swiftwater would start 'em coming and keep 'em coming. 'Swiftwater, Where the Wild Geese Stop!'"

"But they don't always stop," said Hayes, the hotel man. "In fact, only once in several years."

Mr. Fraser braved this out: "They have stopped. They will again. They go over, don't they? Besides, the advertisement's the thing."

It was the undertaker who broke the silence at this critical point. "They tell me Bucky Calloway says he knows why the geese stop some years and not others. They say he brags about it—"

"You don't say," said Mr. Fraser.

"Crazy as his father," said Hayes.

Old Alf cut in with a rabid snort. "It's you fellers an' the town that's crazy, not Bucky Calloway," he cried. "Crazy an' asleep, as our friend Mr. Fraser was saying. Bucky Calloway knows right enough what'll make the geese stop an' it ain't brag-talk neither. Bucky come to me with his idea long gone, an' I gave him a heap o' advice. I an' him are what you might call partners in a little idea concernin' the wild geese. Bucky an' his pa are workin' out the plan right now an' you fellers are like to have your eyes opened to a few things come fall."

Any other man who had gotten back of some plan of the no-account Calloways would have been laughed down and pooh-poohed to silence, but not a man present but would as soon have poked a fire with a stick of dynamite as cross Alf Simes. Alf talked on for a time, alluding to Bucky Calloway and his project, but refusing to lift the veil that overhung the matter. Mr. Fraser listened with an intensity that precluded even the asking of questions, for he knew that if Bucky Calloway knew what made the wild geese stop, maybe he knew how to make them stop.

The night was unseasonably warm for the time of year. Upon retiring, Mr. Fraser lay wakeful by the open window. His sporting blood had been roused and his thoughts stimulated by the talk he'd heard and the memory of the geese on the lake. Vaguely he longed for some nameless freedom, weary as never before of toting heavy bags of hinges and doorknobs and ever-thickening catalogues from town to town.

He fell asleep at last and toward dawn he wakened suddenly and the idea was still there, clear as glass. He could write his own ticket. He could see the alluring advertisements; hear men talking about it in dozens of distant towns. It was a bonanza of an idea; it would carry him far. But he must find a man with the know-how.

Next morning he asked some cautious questions here and there. In the afternoon he rented a horse and rig and drove out along the lake-shore road toward the Calloways' marshland cabin.

It was a strange meeting in more ways than one. As Mr. Fraser was tying his horse to a tree, a great dog rushed out and set up a fierce brawl. Mr. Fraser, however, was somewhat of a dog man and soon had the animal mollified. But as he was approaching the cabin what should come barging out of the thickets but a full-grown bear, his great mouth agape in what was evidently a savage snarl of challenge. Keg had come upon the new Calloway cabin only the day before and had won a lasting truce with loneliness. The new cabin became synonymous with the old to Keg and it was as if his long and lonely vigil had never been.

Rearing and whinnying in terror, Mr. Fraser's horse broke free and fled, buggy and all, some five hundred yards into the forest. Pudgy Mr. Fraser himself turned and ran, his face gone the color of an old lime wall. He was yelling at the top of his voice, when Cam Calloway appeared. To Fraser's amazement he drove off the bear with a stroke or two of a switch. Then Bucky came out of the cabin, almost man-grown now, hardly recognizable as the boy of the fall before.

"I'm right sorry that fool bear had to go an' scare you," Cam apologized. "He looks right fractious, I'll swear, but he's harmless as any cow animal. Just a pet we raised up from a cub."

"A pet!" panted Mr. Fraser. "Sweet Jesus and General Jackson!"

When he had regained his breath, the three went up to the cabin. Very cautiously Mr. Fraser led up to the subject of the wild geese, but soon Cam and Bucky were talking freely. The perennial dreamer in Cam was met and matched after a fashion by the perennial long-chance gambler that lived in Dell Fraser. All that Cam knew and told about the geese only bolstered Mr. Fraser's rosy plan, though the interests of the two were wide apart as the poles. The Calloways signified neither interest nor dispassion in the salesman's long, wordy pictures of what a wild-goose sanctuary might mean to Swiftwater. They simply heard the other out, endured it as rocks in a stream endure the swirling waters round them. Mr. Fraser might do what he liked. Safety for the geese in the near-by marshes was all that concerned the Calloways.

Mr. Fraser quickly changed his tactics. He talked nothing but sanctuary after that, but led the others out on ways and means. When they parted the three were copartners in silence on the vaguest long-shot gamble any of them had ever hoped up, even in fancy. More corn was to be planted at once and Mr. Fraser left with the Calloways a hundred dollars in cash—a sort of grub-stake agreement, more to come, later when needed—for the things they might want for the furtherance of the plan.

That night Cam and Bucky went into town to pay a few bills. In spite of the big new idea, Cam's spirits seemed low. It had been so since spring. Cam carried on, but he talked little these days and his back was bent a bit as though he carried a heavy load. Not all Bucky's talk about the geese and the possibility of a permanent living for Cam if the sanctuary was established seemed to brighten his father's outlook. Something worked on his mind; it would come out when it suited him, Bucky thought.

It was as they walked home under the stars that something of it came to words.

"Like to see Peter Nigosh again. Hunt him up, maybe. That hawk dream o' mine—been naggin' me all week. Fair boogerish it's got to be. Last night in my dream I lay in a rocky, fearsome place, held down hand an' foot, with the cussed bird tearin' at me. Could hear it scream—"

The words struck into Bucky, opening up a nest of fear. A darkness in them; 'twas as if he'd been fearful of hearing them spoken all along. If only it didn't drive Cam away.

"Oh, Pa, it's like a sign," he cried. "You been all changed since spring—" Under the saving cover of the darkness Bucky's heart and dread seemed woven with his words. "Please don't go off nowhere this summer. Promise you won't, Pal?"

Cam chuckled quietly. "I got nary mind to leave, son. We'm purely whittled out a job fer ourselves here—us an' Mr. Fraser." He laid a soothing hand on Bucky's shoulder for a moment and a world of apprehension stilled in the boy's chest.

They walked on for a time in silence. Bats rent the evening's porcelain in zigzag lines, like a crack in a cup. Presently it was Cam's turn to loose a shaft.

"The love quill's entered you, son," Cam stated quietly, apropos of nothing. "It's buried deep."

Bucky stiffened.

"I felt it long gone," Cam said. "Knowed 'twas nigh time. Is it the right girl? That's what matters."

Still Bucky could not speak.

"Remember, son, a Calloway's woman's his heart an' life. Never heard tell of a lukewarm one in all our line. Make sure the quill don't break—that's all."

He paused for a moment, then swept away all final barriers with another chuckle. "Oh, it's a fine girl Jeth Mellott's raised an' no mistake. Bridie runs deep. Like us. You showed more'n a grain o' sense there, Bucky. 'Twas more'n chance that made you two hold together, growin' up."

A sweet thrill shot along Bucky's spine at very mention of her name. Oh, thankful he was now for the enshrouding dark. 'Twas to be expected Cam would know. How could it be otherwise? Cam couldn't help knowing, as he knew the spirits of woods and places. Still, Bucky could bring up no words.

They walked on in silence through the warm dark.

23 ~~~~~~~~~~~~~

$\mathcal{I}$N JULY SUMMER SET IN IN EARNEST. THE SUMMER world was the insect world, for no insect ever found a day too hot. The more relentlessly the sun beat down, the faster whirred the wings of wasp and bee and dragonfly. The ants moved faster and the long-faced, armor-plated "hopper-grasses" ate many times their weight of green each day. All month it did not rain. The pinewoods went tinder-dry. 'Twas a real old-time "hot snap," as Ma put it.

Day and night the crickets sounded their eternal note of peace in calm inaction. And among the reeds and bulrushes of the marsh, nesting bittern raised an occasional dry, metallic cry that was for all the world like the rattle of a long chain falling back link by link upon its own coils.

Corn weather, hot short nights. It became clear what the saying meant—that you can hear corn grow. Corn was racing for its life against the weeds apparently, in the Calloway cornfield; another small field not planted till early July struggling up beside it.

August came. All through the hot weather Bucky sulled

and mooned. So little to do, with the woods all somnolent, the creatures somnolent, too, hunting days still far ahead. Neither he nor Cam was ever cut out for crops of corn and beans and rutabagas and pens of chickens. It took more than a sorry farmer to make a go of trap line and hunting trail.

The waiting and inaction made it hard—this big idea of theirs—the goods they had undertaken to deliver to Mr. Fraser. Nothing to know for sure till fall. If it didn't work out, Bucky decided, he might pack up and get out of here. See some of the world as Cam had done. He was old enough now. And then Bridie could have Whit Turner.

Again and again he gave her to Turner, or gave them to each other and welcome, but that didn't settle it. The thing was hot and sick within him, back and forth, always two sides to it. She and Whit never could make each other out though. They would never get along to amount to anything. Bucky knew all about her, as he knew about the wild geese. But his thin lips smiled miserably and he jeered at himself.

"Maybe I don't know so much," he thought. "I don't even know if the geese'll stop—if they'll even come over." A host of uncertainties kept him frightened and feverish.

And then one day he actually talked with Bridie and things were changed a bit. She overtook him on his way to town, with quick, almost noiseless steps, after he'd passed her place.

"Hello, Bucky," she greeted, and fell in beside him.

"Hello," he said huskily. Then he went dull, his thoughts taking a perverse turn now that she had bridged the distance between them.

"Going in to Stemline's?" she asked.

"Yes."

"You never stop by any more," she said, and his heart gave a flip like a hooked salmon.

"Had no time," he said.

"Father said at breakfast that he hadn't seen you in months."

"I've seen him."

They were silent for a space, walking close, each in a wheel track in the winding road. He smelled the clean fragrance of her. His head was swimming, but all the anticipation, all the things he'd planned to do and say were lost in a hazy dreaminess. By the Lord, if a sort of sleepiness hadn't fallen over him. They walked with quickened pace now, but stuck in a mud of silence, as if they'd just met inopportunely. Once or twice she looked up at him intently.

"How's everything at your house?" she finally said.

"All right." A happiness was welling up in him, but he couldn't speak. Something weighed him down like lead. A lot of senseless things rose to mind and each as it was thrust back made everything harder, till he went red and swallowed. Oh, he was the biggest fool that ever wore shoes, not a doubt of it.

"Bucky—"

"What?"

"Don't you know that people are all wondering and laughing about your cornfield and the way you let it go untended?"

"I've heard it—seen it, too," he said.

"Why don't you and Cam plant the way the others do, Bucky? Then they'd stop."

"We got our reasons."

"I knew you must have. Father said so too. Said he wouldn't wonder if Cam had just put in some corn for the woods varmints. But it's all made me mad."

Silence again, but his pulse was quickened, his blood surging in the knowledge that she'd been concerned.

"You never go into town Saturday nights, do you?" she asked.

"No."

"There are parties, and sometimes a dance at Town Hall. It's lots of fun."

"I suppose Whit Turner takes you to 'em," he burst out. He said more. Plenty of words he found when it came to bitterness. He could scarce bridle them back.

"A girl can't just sit at home forever," she said when he had finished. The words were quiet, but it was like a hot nail back for him. Her face was partly turned away. "Did you know that Whit Turner hasn't forgotten about last fall? He's been waiting and fixing ever since for another fight."

"Did he tell you that?"

"No. But he's been training, they say. He's got a punching bag. Aren't you scared?"

"Guess I can take care of myself."

"Could you, if it wasn't over the wild geese?" Cam had said almost that, he remembered.

"Why do you care so much about it—think I'll lammux him again?" he burst out.

"Oh, it's none of my business, of course," she said. "I just thought I'd tell you."

Then they came to the town edge and parted, going different ways. He'd muddled everything up again, he guessed, and a new wretchedness enveloped him.

Once only Mr. Fraser had come out again, rather surreptitiously, to the Calloway place. There was another long talk; there were a few additions to the plan; another strip of corn was to be planted that would ripen by late fall. Mr. Fraser had gone cannily into the matter of protected areas. He suggested that a tame decoy goose or two be procured as a lure to the flocks, but this Cam would not consent to. The geese would come without tricks, he said.

Bucky felt better after the visit. He had been tending

to his end of the bargain, Mr. Fraser had, stirring things up in town, dropping seeds in the Swiftwater mind. He'd been showing up weekly in town, not confining himself wholly to the hardware trade. There'd been business with the bank, careful talks with leading citizens. Life had trained Mr. Fraser in the slowness of budding monetary affairs, but the slowness of Swiftwater was a perennially painful experience. He saw with unshakable clarity that Swiftwater was his future field of operation, saw that the town couldn't sleep forever, that tourists, a railroad spur, a paved highway even, were destined to connect it with the cities to the south. But even he had no idea of how slow his project would be to sprout.

One of his best bets, the projected Lake Shore Highway, had met with complete resistance. Swiftwater feared the taxes; a goodly part of the leading merchants were frightened cold at the thought of taxes. Moreover, Swiftwater seemed unable to see that the wild geese could have anything to do with the town's future. That part of Swiftwater which was without funds could see it, but Swiftwater of the buttoned pocket was not so romantic.

Many of the details Mr. Fraser did not report to the Calloways. It had become apparent that the only real enthusiasm over the wild-goose plan came from Swiftwater's sporting element, who saw possibilities for unlimited hunting ahead and the chance to draw in city hunters. At this stage of the game Mr. Fraser was not objecting to any interest whatsoever; in fact, the latent hunter in his own blood had been roused. Hayes of the Lakeview expressed the general opinion:

"You can't keep people from shooting at a goose flock as it goes over. I know how they feel. Every time I hear 'em cackle up there the palm of my hand itches for the old shotgun. I'm just pulled to the gun rack. It's human nature. I don't guess the geese mind it a lot either."

"When the town realizes that them are the geese that laid Swiftwater's golden egg—" Mr. Fraser said with oratorical fervor. Suddenly his mind lit with the power of his last words. "The Golden Egg," he repeated. " 'The Golden Egg,' gentlemen, that's the name for this big new hotel—golf, tennis, saddle horse, beach proposition I've been talking of. 'The Golden Egg that the wild geese laid,' we can explain as we pass out candles to our guests retirin' at night—" He glanced around, but his facetiousness was quite lost on the hangers-on.

"But they don't lay anywheres hereabout," said Hamey the undertaker.

"As to that," said Mr. Fraser, with a foamy light in his eye, "I have reason to believe—strange as it may seem, I have reason to believe it can be fixed."

Later Postmaster Briscoe had exploded: "Fixed for the geese to stop an' layl Fraser's a live wire all right, but he might's well tell me he's contracted for an orchestra of trumpeter swans to play each evenin' on the hotel porch."

Still Mr. Fraser was getting his idea into action, though considerably delayed, and all on his own funds and initiative so far, or so he thought. It was some time before he became aware of a powerful ally working for his cause. He learned of it from Bucky Calloway. Old Alf Simes had been getting in some work on the Swiftwater public mind. At first Mr. Fraser was racked with misprision about this. Old Alf was a cute one; it could be he was cutting in on the plan for his own ends. It was not until an evening in mid-August, when a small group of the town businessmen consented to foregather at Town Hall and hear all he had to say, that his mind was set at rest on that score. Old Alf himself appeared at the meeting just as Mr. Fraser got up to speak. Alf was dressed up till his own mule wouldn't have known him.

The hardware man put forth his arguments pro and con. There was the usual lukewarm reaction from the assembly. But before the luke had cooled to a definite chill, old Alf himself got up and took the floor without so much as by your leave. Where Mr. Fraser had given out bald statements of fact, old Alf executed some clever flank attacks, drawing upon the powers of eloquence, persuasion, and imagination. He skirmished skillfully, driving home his points under cover of humor, needling his listeners now and again with sharp sallies that apparently shamed a few, working from the vantage of a lifelong knowledge of their ways and weaknesses, things Mr. Fraser could never come by.

Alf talked on for twenty minutes and as always a sort of mesmerism began to work on his listeners. Somehow the word had gotten round, and men began slipping in at the open door, one and two at a time, eager to hear anything Alf said. Before long folk were crowding the hall thick as flies and as always Alf's craft was whetted by numbers.

Two things stood out for Mr. Fraser: First, that old Alf had nothing personal on the ball. He was arguing the case of the wild geese mainly out of contrariness, because he knew it was unpopular. Second, Alf was stumping the straight Calloway ticket; it was purely the sanctuary idea, no shooting, no outside hunters coming in, that Alf argued for. Well, let him. Anything that would get the idea started would serve the purpose. Once the town got behind the idea and the geese started coming, human nature would take its course. There'd be hunting aplenty—no one could stop that—and the Fraser plans would work out, whether or no. Business was business, and old Alf had turned out to be his ace in the hole.

But Alf was drawing up his big guns for the kill. "You men can't get the idea of huntin' out o' your heads. You're hindsighted like you always been," he accused.

"You want to see city duck hunters swarm in here spring an' fall for the mite o' money they'll drop while they're in town. 'Twouldn't be long 'fore the flocks was killed off an' then where'd you be? If you got the geese to stop an' protected 'em, 'twould soon draw tourists from all over the country. Science sharps an' even the Government would soon take notice of you. 'Twould be the makin' o' the town.

"This is a Swiftwater project, men, an' Swiftwater's got to keep control of it. Now let's us consider this little meetin' as the first assembly of Swiftwater's Chamber of Commerce. Here we stand tonight under one o' the wild geese's overland routes. This is the place where you hear 'em an' see 'em, goin' over an' out on the lake. Yes, sir, we got the key to public fancy right here in our hands. We even got the slogan, the key line, as our friend Mr. Fraser put it, that'll start this town goin' an' keep her goin'. Let's us decide right now which way we're headin'.'"

There was prolonged discussion. But still the general vote was against giving full sanction to the idea at present. But people would weigh the matter; they would wait and watch. All of it depended on what happened in the fall migration.

Corn was ripening now. Already many of the farmers were at their cutting. But the scraggly field of fodder on the Calloway place still stood high above the mats of weed—kernels filled out and toasting brown in the sun; a second field was just beginning to ripen.

"Of all crazy things!" People still had their say and laughed, for few had any idea that the crop was not for the Calloways' own consumption.

And now a change was beginning to be felt in all the forest. You could see the signs of it here, and there, and everywhere, if you'd the woods eye. An unwonted stillness in the underways for the time of year, fewer birds, a growing dearth of the rabbit folk. It was as if Nature had sickened of her long prolificacy and turned her face away.

Often one came upon a rabbit or a bird lying dead in the thickets for no known cause. Often the Calloways saw rabbits and birds that were plainly sick and enfeebled. Once a weasel passed through their field. His red-brown fur looked dry and scrofulous, his eye was glazed, and he'd lost his marvelous speed and litheness, but he was carrying out to the end the mission for which he was born, the injunction fate had put upon him to kill.

"That feller's near his end," Cam said. "Mind what I told you last fall about the Die Off, Bucky? Oh, it's workin' fast. All through the woods the critters are sick an' dyin'. We'll see but a handful of pa'tridge this season. Owl an' hawk an' wolf an' panther'll fatten on the weak this year."

"What'll it do to the geese, Pa? Think they'll stop this year?"

"I got a right smart feelin' they will," Cam said. "The death time'll not affect the geese. They live in the law; they never overbreed. It's the critters that'll suffer most. By winter, followin' a trap line'd fair beggar a man. He'd scarce get enough hair for his eyebrow."

"What'll we do come cold weather?"

"For once, son, I don't rightly know," Cam said.

Ordinary folk sensed nothing of all this, nor ever would, except that they'd go out grouse hunting that fall at the usual time to the appointed place and for some mysterious reason return empty-handed, where in other years they'd filled their bags. But over in the Indian village the Micmacs knew what to expect. All summer the old men had talked of it. The Tenth Year of No Rabbits had come again, the great tidal wave of death in the forest. The tribe would lay by what fish and smoked meat they could against the inevitable lean time, but before winter was over, they knew, there'd be many a cinched belt among them, unless Government stepped in to aid them.

PROPERTY OF
FRANKFORT SCHUYLER CENTRAL
HIGH SCHOOL LIBRARY
FRANKFORT, NEW YORK 13340

24 ~~~~~~~~~~~~~

CAM WAS NOT GREATLY SURPRISED WHEN A MR. JAMES Fretcher sought him out for a guiding trip at the end of August. It was far too early for any hunting, as Cam pointed out, but Mr. Fretcher waved that aside.

He came out with a friend in a big high-powered car to the end of the lake road, and the two of them had tramped the rest of the way to Cam's cabin. They brought with them a note of introduction from Dell Fraser stating that they were old friends and urging Cam to do all he could for them during their stay in the country. They would be of help later on the idea of the wild-goose sanctuary.

They were two of a party of five, they explained, out for a few weeks in the woods. Until legitimate hunting began, they wanted Cam as a sort of camp factotum, to manage the cuisine, as Mr. Fretcher put it, at ten dollars a day.

"The same wage will continue right on through the deer and grouse season and there'll be a nice little bonus for you at the end of the period," Mr. Fretcher said expansively. "Fraser'll tell you any man who works for me is treated right," he affirmed.

Cam was not taken with the idea, nor with Mr. Fretcher, a red-shaven, meat-fed individual with a hard eye and a brusque, impatient manner. But Fretcher was a forceful man, used to getting what he wanted. Besides, such pay was not lightly to be disregarded. Knowing Cam's ever-present impecuniousness Dell Fraser had banked on this. Cam finally accepted.

On the stream bank, five miles north of town at the end of all roads, Mr. Fretcher's party were encamped, if the word "camp" could be used to designate such an entourage. There were three large, mosquito-proof tents in process of erection when Cam arrived and a great bird hunter's blind, which had been hauled in and half sunk in a reed bed at the stream's edge. This affair was already becoming the wonder of the countryside; folk had been coming for miles around to gape at the contraption. It was a master-built marvel that rolled on wheels, finished in aluminum and rubber, with shelves for provisions, folding beds and tables, a built-in ice chest, and wall lights, operated by electric dry cells—roomy and finer far than any cabin in the region. Its grass-camouflaged roof lifted up by a lever for quick wing shooting. It contained an arsenal of shotguns in racks. Cam had never dreamed that such a thing existed, and was sorry to find it did.

A young woman in white shorts sat sunning herself before one of the tents. This was Fretcher's daughter, Dorothy. Two men sat laughing and talking in the blind on cork-cushioned chairs, with tall glasses in their hands and a damp mist of evaporating gin on their flushed faces. These were introduced to Cam by Mr. Fretcher. One, named Beckett, was a fleshy, coarsely friendly individual with the shine of crockery blue in his pale eye. The other man, Twining, was lean, blasé, and rather sardonic. Mr. Delford was the youngest of the party. All were cordial enough, but there was cold beneath their effusion, a gulf between them and Cam that would never be bridged. Not a real hunter in the lot. Most any man along the Swiftwater had forgotten more about the woods than these people would ever know.

Cam made a lean-to camp for himself after his own fashion, well apart from the rest. He saw at once he had undertaken a superhuman job. The work was easy enough, but Cam was never cut out to be a camp cook. He had the tempers as well as the temperaments of the party to deal with and all these city people were a total loss to the great outdoors. Their very noise drove back the elements they had come to find in the woods.

Instinct counseled Cam to draw out of the situation the first day. But there was his allegiance to Dell Fraser to think of, and he had already committed himself by spoken word. He would see it through, for it also meant a winter grub-stake at least. And who would ever have dreamed that these strangers symbolized the sword that had hung low over his head for four months past?

During the long idle days that followed, the party fished, drank much liquor, and listened to their raucous portable radio—that ensign of their civilization, that reassuring emblem of their city identity which drove back the spirit of the deep woods a bit farther each day. Dorothy Fretcher, in her white shorts, hair prettily tumbled under a cork helmet, played at roughing it about camp. When she went a few hundred yards up or downstream she wore high boots and slung field glasses over her shoulder.

Each day she and Mr. Delford resumed what was evidently a blasé amour of long standing. They played prettily at it, here, there, and everywhere, to the obvious approval of Mr. Fretcher. It included brazen caresses, love calls, and the bright patter of give-and-take.

"Flora and Fauna," Twining aptly named them.

All of this was for public consumption, like a part they fell into. Dorothy was the moving spirit of it. When the two were off alone, Cam observed, they were coolly oblivious to each other.

It was apparent that Cam was expected, among other things, to entertain the party with hunting stories and anecdotes of the wild during the long evenings round the campfire. Cam was a master taleteller, but his arts did not flourish in this company, to Mr. Fretcher's annoyance. In more ways than one he was not the sort of handyman these men were used to: that mixture of toady and sharpster that could consolidate itself in the good graces of the venal business mind. Cam maintained a reticence and an Indian pride that were antagonizing to men used to buying cheap and selling dear. The city takes orders from those who pay and Mr. Fretcher was very used to giving them. Many an order issued in vociferous impatience Cam chose to ignore as a mere matter of pride, fighting down an irritation that amounted almost to active hatred for the party and the whole project in hand. Cam was unused to men who believed money could do everything.

He took to wandering off from camp whenever the opportunity presented, feeling an urgent need for getting out of range of his employer's voice. Sometimes he was able to drop by at the home cabin and confer with Bucky on their plan. And sometimes Bucky would stop at the river camp, but his visits were always brief. He had Cam's reaction to these city folk. Each time he went away with a sense of trouble in his breast, but 'twas a trouble he could not put words to.

One day Dell Fraser drove out to the camp. He was greeted with loud cries from all the party and haled into the blind, where he remained for several hours. There was prolonged talk and laughter and much drinking that afternoon and when Mr. Fraser took his leave he was considerably more than three parts drunk. He stopped for a minute to speak with Cam.

"Cam, my boy," he said, "our plan's working. It's working fast. This is only a beginning. The world's going to know about us out here, in spite of the thickness of the timber and the Swiftwater public skull. We're going to see ourselves on the map. Just carry on."

The contact left Cam with a deep and growing doubt concerning Mr. Fraser and even the plan itself, but he did not speak of it to Bucky.

Thus several weeks drifted by and deer season came. Mr. Fretcher and party wanted some venison. They also wanted a few heads to mount as trophies: the head of a stag, for instance, and a panther and a lynx; a timber wolf and if possible a moose. Obviously they expected Cam to produce all these killers without delay and in the same locale. The disclosure that there was no virgin hunting ground where all these beasts hobnobbed together and that days or weeks of waiting and tramping must be entailed with each kill was almost too much for Mr. Fretcher.

By dint of great patience, and a craft that would have taxed the strategy of Hannibal, Cam managed to convoy three of the blundering party on a successful deer hunt. A six-tined buck lying by the campfire that night and the savory odor of venison for supper revivified the spirits of all.

Mid-September had come now, bringing the first grouse and wildfowl winging southward. As is often the way with neophytes in the woods, it was next day, when they were quite unprepared, that Mr. Fretcher, Beckett, and Delford discovered that the Swiftwater woods held bigger and fiercer game than any of them cared to reckon with. They had spread out at Cam's orders to walk up some grouse when a sudden exclamation from Fretcher jerked Cam round.

"Hounds of Babylon! Look at that!"

About a hundred feet away from Fretcher stood a big bull moose, motionless, with its gaunt head and forequarters half masked in the undergrowth. There are times when a bull moose drifts through the densest cover with no more sound than a stalking cat. It is then that he is really dangerous.

It was old Lophorn himself. Another fall had come round, again something had been keeping Lophorn from the side of the mate Nature had intended for him, and he wasn't sure but what it was Mr. Fretcher. His little eyes glowed red with suspicion.

"Don't shoot!" yelled Cam. "It'll only make him branfired mad. Back up quiet toward this tree. If he charges, run an' shinny up it." He indicated a low-branched spruce as Fretcher glanced behind.

Fretcher complied while Lophorn watched, getting madder by the moment. Fretcher was twenty feet from the spruce before the bull made up his mind. With a wrathful bellow he came pounding across the glade between.

"Run," shouted Cam. He was already at the tree and hoisted Mr. Fretcher aloft, swinging up after him with not an instant to spare as the moose swept beneath them.

Beckett and Delford had likewise climbed near-by trees. For the next two minutes the big bull put on a pantomime of murder and mayhem below them that made the city men quake. The lower branches of the trees in which the men had taken refuge were whipped, the thickets round about trampled down by Lophorn's big, splayed hoofs. Cam chuckled as he watched, thankful that Lophorn's perennial luck was with him once again, for not a man of the party carried anything but a shotgun.

How long the men might have been held aloft as prisoners there is no saying, had not a ruse come to Cam. While Lophorn was shaking his antlers beneath the high perch of Mr. Delford, some thousand yards away, Cam cupped his hands to his mouth and uttered a soft, strange call, a crafty imitation of the cry of a cow moose seeking a mate: "Who-aah, who-aah."

The big bull's fury fell away. He swung about, long ears erect to catch a repetition of the call. It did not come, even when Lophorn sounded an answering call. Surely he had heard that soft and timorous plaint, though from what direction he could not tell. All thought of the men banished from mind, Lophorn drifted off among the trees, stopped, sounded a second and more imperious summons, then went crashing away.

When the sound of his going had died away the men climbed stiffly down from their perches, but the idea of grouse hunting was quite gone from every head. Mr. Fretcher was high-fire now on the subject of moose. He fancied that after having nearly been trampled to death by a bull there was no further doubt in anyone's mind but that there was big game in these woods. He toyed sarcastically with the subject, oblivious to the warning flush beneath Cam's tan. He was a city man, he said, but he generally got what he went after. He would pay Cam two hundred dollars for another chance at a bull moose with a magazine rifle instead of a bird gun in his hands. He wanted action in the big-game line, and he wanted everyone to know it.

"Sure you do," Cam said quietly, and moved on campward.

Next morning the idea of a moose hunt was dropped, for the first wild ducks were heard quacking on the river. Every member of the party was ignited. Guns were oiled and put in order, decoys were unpacked, and Fretcher ordered some special phonograph records tried out. These were to serve as a lure to the birds. Young Delford put a record on the machine. *Quack, quack, quack*—a guttural medley of excited duck voices filled the air. Cam would have sworn, had he not stood watching, that the stream was swarming with feeding mallard. He resented this mechanical trickery.

The following day the bird season officially opened. That morning the party was astir before dawn. Breakfast was hurried and before the night mist had lifted from the stream the men were stationed in the blind, the grass roof lifted. It was still dank and cold and each man had a nip or two of whisky to fortify him. The blind was filled with the reek of bourbon.

"Have one, Calloway," Fretcher grunted.

Cam shook his head.

They proceeded to instruct Cam in the art of gun passing. Each man had three guns ready: short-range, middle-range, and long-distance. Cam was to stand watch over the extra guns.

"When one of us reaches back, like this, hand him a gun," Fretcher said.

"Mallards!" called someone presently. "Drop the roof."

Delford pulled a lever which let down the grass top and the four men took shooting positions. Fretcher had set the decoy record going. Through the openings in the blind they could see the river from three sides.

A tattered flight of mallards came whistling over, dipping down through the mist to discover the source of the quacking. They were nervous and circled again. Around they came once more, necks stretched low and eager. Then they saw the floating decoys. The whistle of wings ceased on the instant; tail rudders snapped down, and they planed sharply toward the water.

From two sides of the blind, fire and thunder burst forth. Scatter loads and choke loads ripped and tore

the flock to pieces. Cam thrust extra guns into four
back-stretched hands as the remnant of the ducks
climbed steeply up from the trap. Four more birds
dropped. Grunts of satisfaction went round.

These men were trap shooters par excellence, Cam
saw; their chief pleasure was fast wing shooting. At this
they were good. But he stood gazing in puzzlement and
annoyance as the men poured fresh drinks while the
dead birds floated swiftly away downstream. Within two
minutes the current had drawn the floating ducks round
a bend, all but two near shore, which young Delford
brought in with a pole.

A half hour later it was the same when a flight of teal
went skimming low above the water with flickering
wings. The flock was blasted, almost exterminated, by
the first fusillade of the repeating guns. Cam stood waiting in growing anger for the men to retrieve their kill.
A bad smell was beginning to hang over the river woods
for him at this insight into the mechanics of blind shooting. Finally he blurted:

"Ain't you aimin' to fetch in them birds? That lot'll
mighty nigh make your limit."

"Hell, no," said Fretcher.

Cam stood looking at him. Such waste of life and
game was incredible—letting twelve or fifteen ducks drift
away as food for prowling coons and foxes. "Don't you
fellers eat duck?" he said.

"Sure we eat duck," said Fretcher, "but we're out for
shooting. If we picked up all the birds we'd have our
bag limits before noon. What floats downstream can't be
pinned on us. We don't aim to have our bag limits till
sundown, understand?"

His conspiratorial grin was reflected in every face
but Cam's. Cam's jaw stiffened.

"That don't rest my mind none," he retorted. "To you

fellers wild birds are just somethin' to blast at. I don't
like it."

"There's plenty of ducks; always will be," Fretcher
said irritably.

"There won't be long. This kind o' business'll blot
'em out. Don't tell me you do thataway huntin' wild
geese, Mr. Fretcher!"

Fretcher couldn't tell whether it was a bird, a snake,
or a devil that gleamed for a moment in Cam's black
eyes, but his jaw went ugly. He turned to face Cam
squarely, as if trying to submerge the smaller, slighter
man with sheer physical bulk as well as words.

"Now look here, Calloway. I don't pay men to lecture
me. Dell Fraser recommended you as the perfect man
for us—a fellow who knew the woods and could keep
his mouth shut. Our kind of hunting may not be your
kind, but that's strictly our business. We manage to have
our fun and it's no hair off your neck. If we beat the law
now and again, we do it legal—no danger to us or to
you, understand? Just for your peace of mind, your Game
Warden, Fonse Turner, is a close friend of mine. He'll
look the other way when we're around; he knows which
side his bread is buttered. Now I don't like arguments.
Here, have a drink and forget it."

He thrust a tall glass into Cam's hand. In the heat of
the moment, hardly knowing what he did or caring,
Cam raised the glass and drank. His wrath, the slow-
burning anger of the law-abiding, throbbed in his veins.
He drained his glass.

Two hours later found him sitting on a log at the edge
of camp already velvet-drunk, and darkly bent on going
deeper, his mind torn with strange fury and grief, misery, and something akin to suicide. He'd been sold out.
Dell Fraser had shown himself to be a traitor to the
plan on which they had both agreed. Warden Turner
was a part of the hateful setup in which he was meshed.

Some black, annihilating force that had hung poised, suspended for weeks, ready to shoot down an unseen groove, had been released at last. And now Cam himself was the sword that hung low over his own head—hung by the thinnest, most tenuous of threads.

25 ~~~~~~~~~~~~~~~~

$\mathcal{T}$HE WOODS HAD BEEN DRESSING FOR FALL AGAIN. HERE and there along the hardwood ridges a tree already glowed like a bonfire. The chirring of the last crickets and tree toads was a ceaseless, desperate monody, as if they knew well that any night might bring the blight of frost.

A great and sucking loneliness had assailed Bucky in these first September days. Days so tranced and still and beautiful you were on the verge of heartbreak anyhow—air so soft and winy 'twas enough to make dumb things speak. 'Twas always so with him as fall came on, but this year was different, so deep and smothering a feel he couldn't puzzle it out. As if the woods were ghosted. Even Keg had gone away. Past two years old Keg was now, a big and very bearly bear, and with the first tocsin of fall in the air he'd wandered off toward Sugarloaf, answering the first sex call of his kind.

These last weeks Bucky had been sitting it out alone, so to speak, keeping up the marshland place, carrying out the details of the new plan. It was hard with Cam away. He had Ma's doubts to contend with. She cared not a hait if the wild geese stopped or no; her faith had yet to be won.

One still evening, Ma and Viney having gone in to town with a passing neighbor, Bucky was sitting alone in the open doorway. A cigarette glowed in his hand, for he'd taken to smoking a bit of late, to fend off monotony. After a time he heard girls' voices on the wood road—voices that grew nearer. One said quite audibly:

"I am, too. You stay back. I'm going in."

"But there's no light," from another.

"I don't care. I'm going in to see. You two can stay here."

Bucky sat on in his doorway. 'Twas like that other time. In spite of the surging of his blood he was cooler, colder every breath, now he knew that Bridie's step was on his path.

"Hello," she called from a distance.

"Hello," he said, not moving from his chair.

"Oh, Bucky! Why, you're smoking!"

"Better'n chewin'," he said.

She stopped close by, gasping a bit as if breathless. "Don't you ever come to town any more?"

"Yes, when I have to."

"We've all been wondering about you. Isn't your ma here?"

"She went to town. Pa's on a guiding trip."

"But Bucky, don't you know, after all your work here, it's time to cut your corn? The town says you just keep walking round looking at it when it ought to be in the shock."

"The town's interested a whole lot out here, for such a little piece of corn. Sit down, if you want. There's a chair there against the house."

"I thought I'd like to see you. Oh, Bucky, I wish you'd do something to stop people's talk—"

"They'll find out soon enough what we're doing here," was all he offered. There was a brief silence.

"Whit Turner bring you out?" he asked, knowing Whit hadn't.

"No, just two of the girls."

"Oh I forgot. He's out of town, they say."

She let that pass. They were standing in the doorway.

"I thought I'd like to look in, but there's no lamp," she said.

"Draws the bugs."

"You haven't any screens?"

"We get along."

This time she was letting him have all the irritation. He was in that breath of her that he had known ever since the scarlet fever. No one would dream that his blood was racing. Queer to be remote like this, now that she was here. Just a whim of hers to come, he guessed, but then he thought suddenly and very coolly that it might be up to him to make her remember.

One moment her whitish figure was in the dark doorway; the next it was in his arms, his face buried in her fabulous hair. She struggled, but was silent. He began to know a fiery and unprecedented strength. Her silent struggling seemed to bring it out. She kept her mouth covered, fighting him without a sound. Still he knew a queer, unerring power with her; the deft turn of his shoulder moved her face up to his and locked it there. Her lips parted, but still not a sound.

Suddenly he set her free. She stood for a second before him, panting. He could not see her eyes. She tossed back her head to straighten her hair. Her hands passed down quickly to straighten her dress. Then she turned and ran.

Bucky felt sorry. He didn't know why at first—not for catching a girl and kissing her. Still he was sorrier than ever before, the pent-up depression of months sweep-

ing over him. Not a cry out of her. That was it; that was
what was getting him. Maybe she had just wanted to
see him. Maybe she had been lonesome.

Suddenly he sat up. He knew now. It was to keep the
other girls from hearing that she had been so quiet.
Always queer like that, Bridie Mellott. She wanted him
to take his corn in to keep the town from laughing.
She'd warned him once before about something . . . oh
yes, about Whit Turner.

He got up and rambled off toward the lake. He couldn't
stay indoors tonight. He couldn't stay anywhere. He
ranged aimlessly through the soft night. His nerves were
on end and he was miserable, but underneath ran a
threat of ecstasy—the memory of Bridie's lips. Something ancient and foregone in that that struck deeper
with each passing minute, now he was out here under
the countless stars.

It was very late when he returned to the cabin. Ma
and Viney had come home and were asleep, but for
Bucky there was no sleep. He had never felt so low and
hopeless; 'twas as if the springs of his faith had all run
dry. But deep within was still that haunting undercur-
rent at the memory of Bridie's visit. When, toward morning, he did fall into restless dreaming, his mind was
dogged by gruesome visions that were worse than any
wakefulness. Long before dawn he was up and heading breakfastless for Fretcher's duck blind up the river,
drawn there as by a silent call, knowing only that he
must find Cam and talk with him.

Heavy night mists still hung thick and white over the
river bottom, so dense you could scarce see three feet
ahead. But Bucky's feet found old familiar game trails
and despite the dark and the sea of wet smoke swirling
about him he sped along them like a wild thing.

The mist was just lifting from the river, showing the

lacing of night foam swirling downstream, as Cam
emerged from his lean-to. He moved automatically, like
a wooden man. He should have been impotently drunk
long since, by all ordinary standards. But his body still
did everything he asked it; it walked, moved with inex-
orable co-ordination. Ever since noon of the day before the men of the camp had been plying him surreptitiously with liquor at Mr. Fretcher's orders. But
Cam's mind had remained startlingly clear. It worked at
a fevered pitch that matched his overwrought heart and
blood, until his body and its functions became strange
and foreign and empty of him, as some puppet in bor-
rowed clothes.

Though he had not slept that night he had nonetheless voyaged through a world of dream in which time
and place were often lost. Back into the self he had been
the day before, he plunged at times, but always there
were two things working in him at once. Through the
whisperings of yesterday and the liquor peered the
dark, deceitful present, and the pitiful figure he had
suddenly become. This black and hateful thing going
on here among the birds: something should be done
about it, he knew, but he could not yet tell what. In
fear and grimness he shook off the crushing knowledge
again and again; the treachery of Mr. Fraser which he
saw plainly now, the evil of this camouflage and wholesale slaughter, Warden Fonse Turner's part in this law-
less setup that was subtly killing him.

Deeper grew his torment as he fought against illu-
sion and the golden haze of the whisky that hung about
him in a thickening curtain; swifter and shorter grew
the shuttlings of consciousness from dream to present,
across a chasm that was but a minute wide, yet yawned
immeasurably deep. And in the depths of it gaped death
itself, the ultimate darkness, inevitably sucking him
down. Once seen, the mowing fact of it remained en-

cysted in mind, a small black point that not even the creeping paralysis of liquor could deny. . . . This, the tearing hawk of his dream.

By morning his nerves and body were racked to breaking; reality retreated far within; his surroundings were like a distorted dream. For an hour he had lain listening to the many voices of the dawn—first call of snowbird and chickadee, the rousing reveille of a cock partridge in a distant glen, sleepy, guttural talk of the wild duck awaking on the river. Suddenly in and beneath all other sounds the cry of wild geese came through the mist. He was on his feet. There was no doubt; he heard the calls a second time. . . . Geese out on the lake. They had come at last, the geese he and Bucky had waited for so long. He knew a mighty surge of relief; suddenly everything seemed to break clear.

He emerged from the lean-to and moved down toward the water—his ears straining—and holding fast to his vision. He was only a little surprised when he saw Bucky hurrying toward him.

Abruptly, then, the dim dawn world was torn apart by a deafening crash: the first morning salvo of shots from the hunters, already in their blind. As it burst upon him without warning, Cam had his agonized moment of incredulity. Then, with a rending flash, he remembered, knew what he must do. . . . Dead and dying birds—geese—floating unheeded downriver, a prey to mink and marten. Someone had to stop that, put them out of their misery at last. Out into the swirl of mist and water he plunged.

Bucky too had heard that goose talk in the mist. Suddenly he was running, his heart pounding up into his throat. Something in Cam's movements, even from a distance, had filled him with a weight of dread. He shouted as he ran forward, but it went unheard in a second blast of guns from the blind, the fusillade that cut Cam down.

Bucky screamed at the top of his lungs as he saw Cam fall. Then he was hammering wildly at the door of the blind. Men came piling out in wonder. Two of them plunged out to midstream with Bucky, and at last they dragged Cam in. A light was fetched as they laid him down on the bank, all limp and bloody. Bucky took one look, then reeled and fell as dead. One of the hunters caught him in his arms or his head would have struck a rock. They carried him to one of the tents and worked on him, but it was not till old Doc Waters arrived, nearly an hour later, that they finally brought him to.

PART FOUR

26 ....

$\mathcal{F}$OR BUCKY THE DAYS THAT FOLLOWED WERE TRANCED
and strange. They weren't days at all. They were the
timeless bittersweet melancholy of October with frost
fires in the hardwoods. They were the spirit of the deep
woods with the hawk-lift gone, the face of the forest
somehow turned away. They were tramping without
hunting and the endless song of the fall wind in the
pinetops, haunting as death and pain, subtle as grief
that ran too deep for tears. Bucky saw in those days
more than could ever be told by pen or word: saw how
that fierce, fanatical love of his and Cam's had carried
the seeds of death; how the great and silent clasping of
their spirits had somehow shadowed this.

There was the terrible day of the burial. At first Ma
had wanted a town funeral, but Bucky had suddenly
risen up with a fire that could not be gainsaid. The town
that had always stood out against Cam was to have nothing to do with it, he said. Cam should lie nowhere but
in the woods, on the pine knoll up behind the cabin,
and so it came about.

It was that morning that a coroner's inquest had been held over Cam's body. Old Sol Yorke, the Swiftwater Justice of the Peace, had gone carefully into the matter of the shooting. There was the undeniable fact of Cam's intoxication, attested to by four men. And there was the matter of the heavy mist along the river, which had cut down visibility. So Sol Yorke finally pronounced it an accidental death. Not until then had Mr. Fretcher and his party been able to leave town.

Not much in the way of a burial, it was, though all of Cam's personal friends were there. Besides Bridie Mellott and her mother, there were big Jeth, Wiley Meeks, Luke Callant, Alf Simes, Will Nagle. From the town itself no one came but old Doc Waters, nor had any been asked.

It was the Mellotts' wagon that carried Cam from house to knoll, in the rough pine box that Jeth had made. Very quickly it passed across the wood lot and up the hill—an oblong of yellow-gold behind the driver's seat, for the boards Jeth had used were fresh-hewed pine. An Indian-summer day it was, soft and warm and still; blue-black in the pine shade and smoke-blue in the stronger light of the hills.

'Twas Doc Waters who held all ends together that afternoon, schooled as he was in death and grief; and Doc who said a few appropriate words as the box was lowered into the earth, for even Alf Simes' silver tongue was stricken silent. Doc did not read a regular burial service. He just spoke as if talking to some intimate friends out in the woods.

"Well, Cam Calloway is gone," he said. "Gone just a little before the rest of us, that's all. If we could all see a mite clearer than we do we'd see that the time had come for him to go and that things are all right with him where he is. He was a good man, as good as they come, and he was one of the best friends I ever had. I know this, that whatever comes to people after they die, Cam will get the best there is, because he deserves it. Amen."

It was just there, after Doc's voice had ceased and a silence fell over them all, that somewhere out in the nearby woods an old cock partridge began to drum. It was a long one, with nothing left out from prolonged whir of wings to hollow boom, like the ruffle of drums. It started slowly, swelling through the sunshine, mounting to a roll, a blurred thunder of sound.

There hadn't been a partridge call yet that season, but there it was. Every man looked up quickly into the eyes of his fellows, for Nature didn't time herself to a split dramatic second like that for nothing. It was more than a cock partridge beating a log. It was a further accolade for Cam, a requiem of the Red Gods.

Bucky didn't know how he was going to keep standing, with that smothered feel in chest and heart till he gasped to stave off blackness and there seemed not air enough in all outdoors to keep him there and living. But 'twas Ma who broke first, sinking down on the ground to sob tearingly into her hands, with Viney sobbing beside her. That steadied him. He stiffened then, stood still and straight, even through the hollow finality of earth clods falling on the coffin top.

It was not till hours later that he himself broke and then it was alone and far off in the silence of the woods.

For weeks after that, he did nothing but walk the woods from dew to dew, till muscles flagged and failed and thinking flagged with them. Home had become a place of painful, bated silence. He and Ma were wordless in the face of one another's grief; wordless too because of Viney, whose grief had already all but spent itself. Ma's was a thing that knew no end but self-oblivion —grief that would ultimately wash itself away, leaving behind a dulled and muted surface. But his would never

end. In and beneath it there was the gnawing of self-
blame, for it was he who had pushed the whole idea of
the wild-goose sanctuary, in spite of Cam's disfavor. But
for that neither Mr. Fraser nor the city hunters would
have come into their lives and Cam might still be alive.

All things and thoughts came to a total stop those days,
except the act of walking. But in the woods was no re-
lease, for Cam was a living part of them, the overshadowing dream that lay in them. Whether it was bright or
cloudy, he came walking into Bucky's head: a sudden,
poignant, pine-shadowed form, in the crook of his
arm the old squirrel gun, with body, mind, and feelings,
like the soft, malleable earth beneath the trees, not rock
and stone like other men's.

Never would he be through with that; never would it
empty itself out of his heart into the fungus of forgetful-
ness. Never again, he felt, would the old hawk-lift return, for wherever trail or trap line might lead in the
deep woods, winter or summer, sunlight or shadow,
there'd be the haunting picture of Cam and him walking always and wonderfully together.

Times he communed wordlessly with Cam, explain-
ing, forgiving, making many promises. Once, seeing his
own face in the glass, he was terrified. It had gone so
blank and dead; only the eyes living, bare and luminous
and canvassed by dreadful visions. There was pity for
the boy, even in town, and some went so far as to come
out, to offer him paying jobs, but these Bucky refused.
Once in those weeks he saw Mr. Fraser briefly; a painful meeting, even the salesman stilled and stricken. Mr.
Fraser did what talking there was, though Bucky scarcely heard it. Their plan was still working well, Mr. Fraser insisted. Soon they'd have some backing, money behind them. But all this meant nothing to Bucky. It was
only later that he remembered it—like a delayed echo.

It was Doc Waters who helped most of all through

those weeks—an unspoken bond between him and Bucky since the day of the funeral. Versed in the ebb and flow of life and death and grief, Doc was, and he'd made things a lot easier, almost joshing Bucky at first, filling in the emptiness with talk, skilled post-mortem and sick-bed talk perfected through the years. He spoke as though it were the most ordinary occurrence in the world.

"Why, son, death's no more than a stepping from one room into another. We'll all be doing that soon enough —all of us meeting up with old friends and relatives out there and having a big laugh about the misery we lived through. You act as if Cam was gone for good and all, but it's like it is with them woods flowers there." He pointed to a cluster of dried brown stems. "They're gone for this year, but they'll all bloom again in the spring."

It all helped to keep alive that queer numbed daze that was Nature's own protection—until the time came when the boy could rally and take up the fight first hand. You couldn't tell them much at seventeen, Doc knew, but you could drop ideals and suggestions that would tide them through. Unknown to any he kept close tab on Bucky, ready to do all that could be done in case of crack-up.

But crack-up did not come. Change came instead, at long last, slow as the opening of a cocoon. The wild geese were a part of that. In spite of all he continued to watch and plan, his inner tension mounting as migration time came and reached its height. It brought Cam closer. Impossible to think of him as separate from the geese and the plan.

There came days at last when he seemed not always alone. The streams and the wind said the old familiar things. Always the trees and grass and rocks had spoken to him in voices which were nonetheless voices because they were as silent as his thoughts. But now there came a difference. Sometimes the sunlight seemed rarer, as if with an ineffable nearness. He didn't dare think about that; it wasn't a matter for thinking, but sometimes it was as if the old hawk-lift were coming back. Cam was in that. He was in the song of birds, in the bright path of sunlight in the woods. He was in the hour of dawn and the hour of dusk and in all thoughts that were fine and brave. Slowly Bucky was building himself back to hope.

Thus mid-October came. All the other corn in the countryside was long in the bin, but Bucky's still waved like a tattered army of soldiers, bearing weather-brown pennants. One dawn there was heavy frost and a faint blow of snow in the yard—tinkle of shell ice on the water pail. Bucky moved about the dooryard that morning, an ashen streak on his thin jaws where the summer tan had faded. He was worried, for the time was getting short. All through the nights he had been listening, listening. As for sleep, he knew only the shallow edges of it. Half a dozen times in the night he was awakened by a sort of dream that he heard a clanging note in high sky.

He had thought much about the goose talk he had heard in the mist the day Cam died. There were times when he felt that those first dawn cries had been pure imagination. At other times he knew a fear that it might have been the main body of the geese he'd heard, that they'd all gone over and hadn't stopped at all. But in cooler moments he knew it had been but a small chance flock and that the main migration hadn't started yet.

"They're goin' to stop, sure," he would say. Hadn't Cam said so himself? But sickness of doubt went through him again and again, formed of old defeats of his and Cam's, formed of the town's idea of him. One side of him couldn't believe he could win; the other doggedly affirmed that he must.

"They couldn't have gone over without me hearin' 'em

even if they didn't have a mind to stop. . . . But supposin'
they're late this year an' hurry south in the night without
seein' the standing corn . . ."

But something within knew better. "They wouldn't
have to see corn!"

Then a night of blowing rain on the verge of sleet, the
pinetops moaning, rain in the chimney sizzling down to
the bed of the Calloways' fire. Bucky had been lying
down, but couldn't stay. He was standing shivering by
the fireplace when the first faint *ya-honk* jerked him up.
He ran outside. They were straight overhead. He knew
by the sounds that the flock had faltered. He knew they
were circling. The easy honk of the leader rippled in
repetition along his formation lines like the clink in a
shaken chain. Yes, they were circling.

The deep, reassuring pipe of the drake boomed
again.

"They got it now," muttered Bucky. "They're circlin'
again."

Then they were off, but Bucky had foreseen that. They
had circled twice. They might keep on going to Florida,
of course; they might keep going only to the lake.

He was out on the trail then, running through the
rain. It was close to midnight. He curved round the
edge of the cornfield. Down on the lake shore, a mile run,
he came to a stop, panting, steaming, struggling to silence the din in his chest. The rain steadied; his heart
steadied. The cold was closing in on him when the lake
gave up the first sounds of their bivouac. Yes, they were
out there.

"I guess they didn't mean to stop," Bucky panted, "but
the old drake got to thinkin' it over—what we had—all
laid out for him!" Drenched and shaking now, he lingered. Yes, they were still out there talking it over.

Next morning he didn't move from the cabin, nor
would he let Ma or Viney. He watched from the win-

dows. Not a movement in the corn that day, nor in the nearby marsh. Had they taken off south? But toward night he heard them again on the lake.

Next day he waited again, fearful of some interruption, some move on the part of hunters from the town. They were far back in the marshes perhaps, but not a flicker of a wing in the vicinity of his field. Yet again at dusk their voices came in from the water.

Oh, no, they didn't just come and get it. Things didn't break like that. Three nights they were noisy on the lake; three days they were silent in the marshes. On the fourth afternoon, as he lay flat on the hard, cold ground, a little way back of the cabin, he saw them. They were advancing through the thin stalks—heads of a walking vanguard of geese, necks craning and slanting—taking it all in, the full extent of the treasure.

This was it; this was what he and Cam had waited and worked for so long; this the real winning. Why next year he'd be able to scatter corn on the bare ground and lure them in. . . .

A sudden crash of guns. The geese picked up like an explosion, like a whirlwind, whipping leaves and earth with their giant wings, making for altitude at the shortest possible cut. Scattered shot rained above Bucky, then, running past him, men and boys, stopping to fire again at the rising flock.

Bucky slowly rose, grim-faced, a ghost upon his feet. Among those he turned on in fury was Whit Turner, who smiled and laid down his gun.

"Why I been waitin' a whole year for this," he grinned. "Come on."

27 ~~~~~~~~~~~~~~

WHIT TURNER WASN'T STANDING UP TO FIGHT. HE crouched and circled. Bucky's attention couldn't fix on the fighting face that ducked and shifted before him; every faculty was still held to the ruin of his life—the big plan—and he without even a chance to pick up and put together the pieces.

Whit was heavier, different; he crouched and never stood still. There was a passing flicker before his eyes and Bucky straightened just in time for his jaw to miss a blow which his collarbone took with a snap. It was as if his left shoulder and arm had fallen into a fire. Whit must have been readying himself for months. It wasn't like a blow from a fist; it was like an iron slug thrown too fast for eye to follow.

Whit still crouched, never standing up, huddling back, curving round, and when he snapped out of his crouch you never knew how he would let fly. You didn't care much. You wanted only to get this over with, to try and undo the harm that had been done—if the geese hadn't taken off for good. You couldn't even get mad. But you couldn't quit; you couldn't give over, even if your heart wasn't in it and your mind was far away. You had to stick and "give the other fellow satisfaction," as the saying went, as long as you could stand.

He got in a swinging blow to Whit's head, but took one on the jaw in the doing. Whit sprawled, sprang up, and came into Bucky like a pile driver. That jarred Bucky's will; fury shook him at last. He saw Whit all at once as the embodiment of the town and its scorn, of the obstacles standing between him and the working out of his plan, between him and Bridie Mellott. Fighting mad he rallied now to batter down that grinning face, shouting wild things about the geese that were all incomprehensible to those who heard. But even in the heat of it, he could see the other side, too: people had a right, he supposed, to go gunning for geese if so inclined.

Grimly Whit Turner kept coming in and in, never wild, never over-angry, systematically cutting Bucky down with practiced blows of his hard, dry fists. His every blow told; no knowing from which side it was coming.

They fought on like two young bulls in the glory of youth and strength and fury, toiling, colliding, recoiling, half blinded by anger and the rain of blows. Bucky went down, and as he came up there was a sickening laugh from the watchers. Vaguely he sensed the reason. It was the foolish, pawing motion of his left arm, the one through which the stab of fire had darted. It had gone numb, almost useless, but he kept it up as a guard. He was outmatched in skill, in weight, in age, but Whit Turner could never quell him. He might kill him, but he couldn't whip him.

Times they grappled and fell to the ground, silent save for their labored breathing; slipping in mud, beaten by stones as they threshed and rolled. He lost all track of time. The voices of the watchers came subdued now, as from afar. It was if he had fallen into the whorl of some endless nightmare that swept him on and on.

Through exhaustion and into half-consciousness he fought. He was done and gone, if second wind didn't come. Still he dodged and ducked and lashed out with his one good arm.

Three times more Bucky was beaten to his knees, to the ground, and climbed back up again. The last time agony whelmed him as he sprawled on hands and knees. It was Whit's hobnailed boots grinding his hands into the mud. But a couple of the others grabbed Whit and dragged him off. They had a vestige of fair play.

He staggered up and when Whit came in again it was with a wild rush. Whit was white-eyed now in the killing rage that tires itself out. Bucky heard the hard rasp of Whit's breath. Whit was reeling and nearly done. The sight of that brought Bucky back from something like death. He seemed to loom taller. From a crouching position he seemed to spring into a giant. A blow that started from his thigh came up, back, and around and found Whit's neck. He took one in the side of the head at the same instant and went down, a final time. But it didn't matter. . . . A fellow's work all spoiled, a fellow spoiled, too—

Through a sort of mist then he heard Whit's hoarse voice, a sort of sob:

"I'm done. Can't—fight no more."

"He's comin' to," a voice said. "You all right, Bucky?"
He was lolling back against someone's knee.

"Shuh, yes."

Then he was sitting up. All he wanted was to be alone, to reach the cabin and shut the door. A pair of oxen seemed pulling at his left arm. Then the wreck of his plan was rending him again from within. Vaguely he saw Ma coming across the field.

"Lemme 'lone. I'm all right!"

He levered himself up with his right hand, cursing his muscles for letting him down. He couldn't see very well, stood a second or two to get the direction of the cabin; and then started off. Something about him kept them off, an elaborate stillness in the air. The men neither followed nor started back toward the road. They didn't say anything. Each step he was nearer to being alone. He heard Ma berating them all. But a minute now and he'd be alone. He wouldn't hurry for fear it would start them following.

Now the cabin was just ahead. He stopped to rub his eyes. Something was on the doorstep. He thought he was seeing queer. He rubbed his eyes again; it was still there. He glanced back. Some of the fellows were standing at a distance looking his way, but they didn't see what he saw. Others had moved back toward the road. Ma had gone round to the back door.

"They got me whipped," he kept muttering. "Oh yes, the town's got me whipped all right."

It was still there—on the doorstep. It was very large. It was spread out. It had to do with him, with the real meaning of him and Cam. He was wrecked; he must be seeing a thing that wasn't there. He turned again. The last of the waiting fellows had moved away. He took four steps before looking again—a great goose still on his doorstep, spread out, wings dilating like a butterfly, wings stretching, five or six feet across, the body flat down on the threshold.

Now the long gamey head uncoiled, hissed at him; the black beady eyes held electric points of purest white.

"It came home to die," he muttered in wonder. "It knew where to come."

Another step, the wings lifted, whipped the air, raising the body clear. Then he saw what had happened. Its underside was a smear, its footing all shot away. Nothing to take off with. It was like part of him.

He couldn't pass it to get inside. He stood still and something softened him. Something passed between them. He was wrecked, too.

He knew that something must be done. Slowly he moved round to the rear of the house. There was his rifle, there were the ax and the shovel, but he had only one good hand now. There was the sickle. He found it and moved around in front.

They couldn't even finish their killing; they had to leave it for him.

"It won't be long," he spoke aloud, and solemnly closed in.

The great hissing head shot out to him. With what he had left, with much effort, he put the goose to death. The night seemed coming on fast. He let himself down to a sitting posture.

"I got to rest," he muttered, and flopped back.

28 ~~~~~~~~~~~~~~~~

ℬUCKY FOUND HIMSELF IN BED WHEN HE RIGHTLY GOT
hold of his head again. Under the din of his pain, he
lay listening to random talk from the other room. The
secret had been well kept. Very few people had known
that he had been working with Mr. Fraser, and that he
and Cam had planted their field of corn expressly to at-
tract the wild geese, and that just as the plan began to
work a lot of hunters had come along with guns and
spoiled the job.

Now the whole countryside would know. They were
talking it over in the next room. He heard Jeth Mellott's
voice and some of the hunters, who must have come
back to see how badly he was hurt. All year he had
thought about being understood like this. It wasn't so
much after all. Nothing for him to say now. That was a
relief. They didn't expect talk from him. But there was
something he still wanted to know, yet he couldn't quite
think of it. The men were sure taking it out in talk right
now, but the one thing he wanted to know—no one
seemed to care about.

Bucky began to see it clearer. He'd done his part; no

fault of his if things had been spoiled. Now he could light a shuck and leave if he liked. The big plan had maybe been an impossible dream. A fellow had to make a living; a fellow couldn't sit in a cabin by the marshes and lure wild geese all his life. Nothing to keep him here now. . . . Ma and Viney . . . he had to make a living for them, but that living wasn't in Swiftwater now. It wasn't in the haunted woods of the Jackpine Valley, not this year, with the Die Off on. Already there was a woods famine on; you could see it everywhere. Even the squirrels were disappearing.

He took a deep breath, which hurt him more than usual. All settled, looked like, as soon as he could get his legs to working right. Time he saw the world like Cam had.

Then someone was standing by his bunk. Old Doc Waters; however had he got here?

"They haven't gone yet, Bucky!" Doc said. "I knew you'd want to know. They're out on the lake, just as if nothing had happened. Cam told me he aimed to fix up a place for the geese out here, where they could all light down and be safe. I guess that's what you've been working for all along, isn't it?"

Yes, that was what he had to know. Somehow the doc always understood. A fellow could talk regular stuff to him—almost. He'd think that over sometime. He was led to speak now, words, whole sentences even, about his plan, as the doc sat close.

It was a fact; they were still out in the lake. The crash of guns that had gone up from his cornfield in that crucial hour of his life had hurt him so that it had been easy to believe them gone forever. But would they go back to his standing corn? Had he really made a winning? That was what he had to be sure of.

That night and the next they were out in the lake.

Bucky proved that for himself. Night and morning there was the racket of shooting down by the lake shore; yet the geese remained, riding by night in a tattered raft half a mile offshore. It was three whole days before he could definitely know more.

That was the day that changed all life for Bucky. In the late afternoon, standing arm-in-sling by the rear window of the cabin, his lips moved with awe: "Why, they're in there right now!"

There was a long line of them deep in among the stalks, like vague forms on a tapestry. He laughed silently. The canny drake that led the V was an old whip hand. Drop a goose on a doorstep here and there—more goslings waiting south. Corn is corn. Miles and miles of corn waving under their air lanes, all snapped up and put away just as it was ready to eat, but here was a remote acre choking with golden treasure. Yes, he had them coming.

"Why, if I scattered corn out on the hard ground next spring, they'd stop and get it going north!"

Still, Bucky wasn't sure but he was about through with Swiftwater. He hadn't been driven out after all; he had done what he had set out to. But a fellow couldn't spend his life working out an idea. A bird sanctuary would take money and a lot of help, as Cam had said. Yet it was good to feel them in his own grain. With every kernel they ate he knew they were fixing a habit hard to break.

An hour later a pine log glowed red in his fireplace; night was just beginning to fall; Ma and Viney had gone to town again. Abruptly, old Sounder got up with a stifled roar. Someone was coming along the path.

"Oh, Bucky." It was Bridie Mellott's voice.

"What you doin' way out here?" he called back.

"I had to see you."

"What about?"

He shoved a second chair up to the fire as she came in, flushed from hurrying. Something seemed to have happened to him the past few days. Never even in the old days of their woods traveling together, had he been more cool and self-assured.

"I'm all hot now from running," she said. "I came to tell you that a man from the city's looking for you. He stopped at our house and he's been to the stores and the Lakeview asking questions."

"What's he want?"

"He's from the city newspaper. I thought if I could get to you ahead of him, you'd treat him nicer. I saw Mr. Fraser and he said for you to tell him the whole story."

"What does he want to do, write a piece in the paper that'll bring all the duck hunters out here again?"

"He says he's more interested in your idea of attracting and protecting the geese than anything else. What he writes might mean a lot to you and he's waiting at the Lakeview now."

He watched her as she looked away. He had been afraid she would be through with him for life.

"I just want to rest a minute before we go back," she said.

She had taken the chair by the fire. He moved around and behind her. One side of her face was in the lamplight, the other in the shadow. Always she turned up like this when things were doing, he was thinking; always a way of popping up in his affairs. Here she was again, sitting by his fire. How could she sit so easy after what had happened before? She was a deep pool. You couldn't see the bottom of it. One thing was certain, he wouldn't grab her like that again. Oh, but she was downright lovely—"prettiest girl in the whole darn country." No one really knew her but himself. Somehow he'd always thought of her, even in his lowest times, as his separate and particular property, but he was going to leave her alone this time. The shadowy side was just as real, just as lovely, as the lamplit side.

"We mustn't stay," she was saying. "That man is waiting—"

"I'm in no hurry," he said, unperturbed.

Just perceptibly he heard her long breath, saw her eyes on his sling. "Your arm—your neck—they must hurt a lot," she said.

"I'll live through it."

She looked round the room. "To think that when I was here last I didn't really know," she said. "Wasn't it stupid of me not to know what you were doing all the time last summer?"

"Nobody but Mr. Fraser and Alf Simes knew anything about that for a long time."

"I should have known. I always knew your things before—but you got so proud and stand-offish all at once. To think I could fall in with the rest of the town, thinking you—thinking you—"

"And you came out to tell me it was time to cut my corn," he smiled.

"I had to do something—people's talk made me so mad."

He moved round behind her to the shadowy side. He wanted to kiss her again, but held off. He thought his face must give him away, but she sat looking up at him, not even a mite scared at what she saw. Queer she could sit so cool, alone with him. She was looking into him now.

"But you misunderstand me just as bad—" she said.

"How d'you mean?"

"You know how I mean."

His heart gave a surge.

"I had eyes in my head," he said. "I saw you with Whit Turner, heard the talk in town—"

"Oh, Bucky, I tried so hard to keep him away at first—"

His smile twisted with scorn.

"I couldn't just stay at home all the time, and you were . . ."

Just there Bucky got his first good look into the deep pool—no bottom.

"Later I knew you saw us together and I wanted you to," she said. "You kept acting as if I didn't exist. Sometimes I thought you hated me—"

"And that's why you went to meet him at McKay's and had him out to your house?"

"Every time—"

"Even after you were here that night, and I—"

"Yes—"

"Then you weren't mad?"

"At first, maybe—"

"And after that—" It seemed he could never hear enough.

"It wasn't so easy for me to keep believing in you, the way you treated me. And with all the town talking. Sometimes I guess I wondered if you were—if you truly were—"

"Addled an' no' count?" he finished.

"Ye-es."

He watched her break down, knowing all that was back of it. He swallowed the last of his silly pride; a deep joy whelmed him. All along he seemed to have known just how it would be when they finally had it out together. Everything up to now was the past—the sorry way things had had of working round. Bridie was the future, life itself.

"And you had to find out I really was doing something, just like the others," he said.

"Oh, I knew before that—"

213

"When?" he demanded, and the breath went out of him with the single word.

"When I came here the other time. Oh, Bucky, I knew you always; but that minute you kissed me—I knew that no matter what you were—or weren't—that I didn't belong anywhere else!"

Bucky stood erect. "Oh, Bridie, I been such a fool! I was never like I seemed, any of those times. 'Twas all because I was addled with love for you."

The cabin seemed all at once little and absurd, like a shell he had just broken out of. He couldn't breathe in it a minute longer, so big and changed he was.

Change had come over her, too; her big eyes followed him with laughter and a strange light. They seemed to converge in him. She was on her feet, too, with a swiftness he had never seen in a girl. Then she was at the door.

"Let's go now." He could feel her tremble.

He turned back to bank the fire. At the moment of blowing out the lamp, he turned to her in the doorway—early starshine behind her. She was gone. He ran out of the cabin to find her in the great, roomy dark.

29 ~~~~~~~~~~~~~

$\mathcal{B}$UCKY WAS INCLINED TO BE SULLEN AND UNCOM-
municative at the Lakeview that night, when he met the
press in the person of lanky Matt Laird, a newspaper
columnist in his late forties. He was suspicious at first of
Matt Laird's motives, fearing the coming of more bird
hunters of Mr. Fretcher's stamp. But after a few minutes' talk the newsman won his confidence completely.

It was Dell Fraser who had first notified the press, on
the day Bucky had brought about the stopping of the
first goose flock. Matt Laird, as it happened, had a nose
second to none in the smelling out of a unique and far-
carrying story. He had come north immediately to look
into the story of the geese, sensing what might lay beneath it, and he had already uncovered what he had
hoped for: a story with the conflicting angles of the sporting clique and Bucky Calloway, and with scope enough
to rouse many an official in high places. He had talked
first with some of the town businessmen and drawn
certain conclusions. Five minutes after meeting Bucky
Calloway he had seen the other side of the picture and
established the angle he had hoped for.

He and Bucky went down to the lake shore and talked for an hour. All that Bucky and Cam had dreamed about the geese was drawn forth by Matt Laird with sympathy and understanding.

"Yours is the story we want to tell, son," he said. "You're on the winning side. You've started yourself a new honker hotel here that'll stir up the whole country. Tomorrow I'll launch the story. You'll get publicity— the almightiest power on the panhandle—and that will bring you all the help you need. All you've got to do is sit tight for a while and don't talk. Because you've got a rival mobilization against the cause here, or I'm a Dutchman. The town businessmen aren't working for a game refuge; they're out after wholesale hunting."

Like Cam, Bucky had had his suspicions for some time. Much of what Matt Laird said was to him an impossible dream. But instinct told him he could trust this stranger without reservation.

He didn't even tell Ma of what had taken place that night and the next few days he roamed the woods with his rifle, seeing no one, rigidly keeping his mind off the geese. For the first time since Cam's going, he hunted a bit, but the old zest wasn't in it. It was hard to brave the woods. They were all different, changed as he was changed, still haunted for all his surpassing. He thought it was all himself at first; he tried to blame it on the Die Off Year. But underneath, he knew. They would never again be as he remembered them, with Cam a part of them. The whole country had changed. For Cam had been the last of the old true woodsmen, symbol of a time and a life that could not come again.

There were scarcely any partridge to be found this year, but Bucky shot a prime buck the second afternoon, to put away for winter in the smokehouse. Everywhere he went he kept an eye out for signs of old Lophorn, or the cows he had yarded with. But if any calves

had been dropped they and their mothers had departed
into the forests to the north. Bucky also watched for a
sight of Keg, wondering if his old pet had consummated
his fall mating.

It was six days after his talk with Matt Laird before
Bucky went in to Swiftwater again, mainly to get Ma's
mail. He found the town in a minor uproar. Newspapers
carrying the news story were just beginning to arrive.
The town was seeing itself for the first time in the press
columns of the great outside world—held up as in a mirror. As setting for the bird refuge which was the result of
one boy's dream. No less amazing was it to Bucky than
to any of the townsmen.

'Twas not the first time that a man and a town had to
see themselves first through the public press and the
eye of the world. Swiftwater began to glimpse the possibilities and went suddenly all aclamor. Swiftwater had
been just one more backwoods town, lost in the pines
and waterways, but Swiftwater of the lake woods where
the wild geese stopped to feed was an Arcadia, part of
the breath of life of the crowded towns and cities to the
south. The hunters' paradise was forgotten.

Out on the main street men were shouting themselves
hoarse over it all. Loudest were Dell Fraser and Hayes
of the Lakeview. Hayes had worked himself up to the
rag-edge of hysteria. He alone was responsible for the
sanctuary, to hear him tell it.

"Oh, I've told 'em this time an' again," he shouted.
"Ain't I been tellin' 'em for thirteen years, in my hotel
ads an' foldin' literatoor? They're comin' to see it at
last. Now I'll show 'em a hotel here that'll be the talk
of the lake country."

Oh, there was a lot more to the sanctuary idea than
Bucky had ever foreseen, even in his original dream.
And now it was all coming out—results which went be-
yond his wildest hopes. Matt Laird had sprung his news

story at the exact psychological moment to push Bucky's cause and to curtail the hunters' little scheme.

That was not all. There was an assortment of mail for Bucky. Communications from the Fish and Wildlife Service, the Biological Survey, and TVA. Even the government was vitally interested in Bucky's lake-shore sanctuary—eager to stretch forth the long arm of permanent protection and turn the stopover place into a National Refuge and taming ground. The government had long taken note of the diminishing flocks of the game birds. The swans and the cranes had dwindled almost to the point of vanishing. The egret had become almost a memory and the Everglades kite had gone the way of the buffalo and the grizzly. But the great flocks of the wild geese could still be saved, in spite of the fact that fully a fifth of all the migrating geese were being shot by waiting hunters each season.

Already a representative from Wildlife Service was on his way north to look over Bucky's prospect, he was informed. The man arrived the following day—a kindly, gray-haired biologist, well versed in all the ins and outs of establishing protected-game areas. He and Bucky talked for two hours as they tramped the edges of the marshland. For the first time Bucky listened to talk as knowing and sympathetic as Cam's.

The spot the Calloways had chosen was a perfect one the visitor said: far from town, with plenty of unclaimed land surrounding. Some three thousand acres would be needed to assure extended protection, a matter which would be attended to by the Fish and Wildlife people. Yes, the setup was so promising that Bucky could rest assured the project would be put through. It went beyond even what Matt Laird had promised.

"Will there be work enough in it to keep a fellow—a family?" Bucky asked.

"There'll be work for you for years to come, son

Fact is, you'll need a helper or two," the biologist smiled.
He began to talk over ways and means.

"First thing, we're going to send you one or two men
versed in the know-how of luring the wild flocks in.
They'll work with you for a month this fall and come
back again in the spring. There should be some tame
decoy birds at first and in the spring a good many wings
should be clipped to make sure of a summer stay-over.
Some of the birds will be banded as an aid to keeping
track of their migration.

"In the spring we'll send up a tractor for you. You'll
have to put in a good five acres of corn and another
five of wheat, to assure good feeding. Then a deep,
permanent pool will have to be dredged out for the
geese, and the land fenced in. Within a year you'll be
established here as manager of a new wildlife hotel, my
boy, and you'll number your guests into the thousands."

The goose flock was still in the marshes, still in
Bucky's corn morning and night. As the two rounded
back to the cabin in late afternoon, feeding birds were
to be seen moving amid the dry stalks. The biologist
laughed.

"They're getting tame," he said. "It doesn't take long
for geese to adapt themselves to man. We're booked for
a real winning here."

When he had gone Bucky stood for a time, in the wan-
ing afternoon, listening to the faint, contented sounds
amid the corn. No racket of shots tonight. The concept
of the sanctuary had really taken hold at last. Soon duck
and goose hunting would be a thing of the past in this
region, the bird man had assured him. Yes, it was a winning. All he need do was wait. He went in to break
the news to Ma.

Later he took down his Mackinaw.

"I'm goin' out a bit," he said. "I won't be long."

He slipped out the front way, moving quietly round

by the edges of the pines so as not to disturb the geese
Then he circled toward the pine knoll where Cam was
buried. Owllight had fallen by the time he reached the
jagged tooth of rock that marked Cam's grave.

"We did it, Pa," he breathed to the night wind moving
down from Sugarloaf.

Two scalding tears started from his eyes and bounced
off his cheeks, but that was all. He stood for many minutes listening. Then high overhead faint notes came
dropping earthward—the flock, full-fed, on its way back
to the lake. Bird calls weren't just birds' voices, Cam
had always said. Goose talk dropping through the mist
elfin and melancholy as the fall wind among the pines
subtle as heart hunger, haunting and bittersweet as
grief or pain; essence of that wanderlust that had drawn
Cam forth. Oh, it was true; you could mount right up to
the high hereafter on the wild goose's call.

They wouldn't forget. Tomorrow they'd be back again
And next spring there'd be hundreds. He'd have a deep
pond waiting for them then. Cam would know and be
glad. He'd be able to leave now—happy. . . . But no—i
wasn't like that now. In some way Cam had come to
stay with him. He couldn't leave. Cam was rooted in hi
heart like a tree in the good earth.

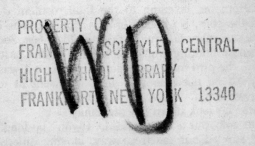

PROPERTY O
FRANK SCH YLE CENTRAL
HIGH OL RAR
FRANK RT NE YO K 13340